AZZARIA

THE DESTRUCTION OF THE FLAMES

NICOLE JAMISON

Also by Nicole Jamison:

AUTHOR'S NOTE

The following book contains torture, foul language, sexual content, violence, and death.

To my dad and those that have been lost, but are never forgotten

MOVYA
MEVIA SEA
NUNOS OCEAN
Teron
KEME
Zakea
MAGEIA
Lake Muzon
Lenia
Mt. Torian
Amura
PYRON
Fajro Entrance
Mt. Trion

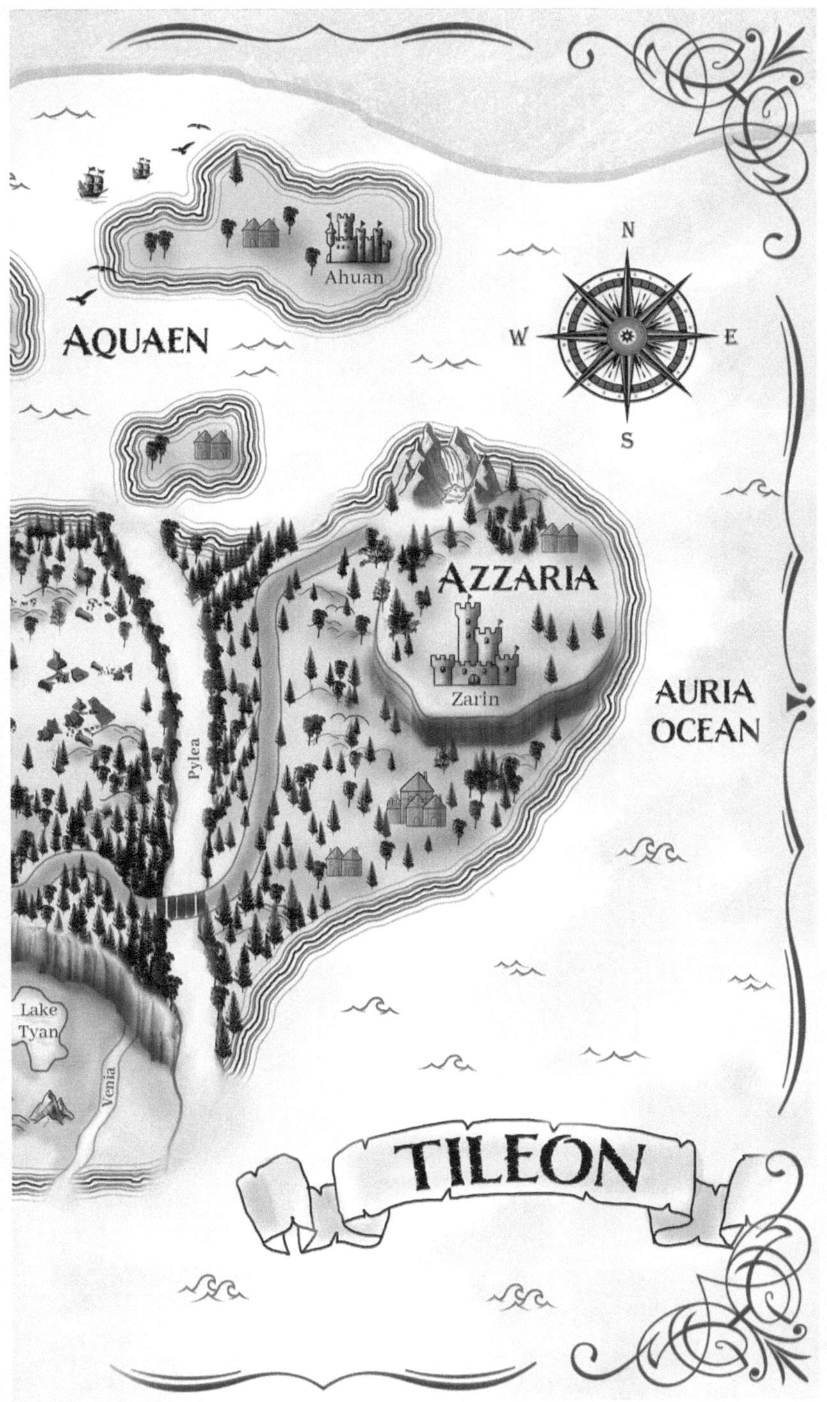

AQUAEN
Ahuan
N
W E
S
AZZARIA
Zarin
AURIA
OCEAN
Pylea
Lake
Tyan
Venia
TILEON

Chapter One

The hot blistering rays of the sun were unforgiving as they beat down on me. I wiped away the sweat that had gathered at the nape of my neck and the few stray drops that ran down my face. The warmth lulled my senses, dulling them into oblivion as the meaning of time slowly fled away. The only notion that the day had begun to pass me by was the darkening of the sky above. I stopped my work and allowed my mind to finally grasp the scene before me.

Dirt covered hands shook ever so slightly, a sign of the internal struggle I was battling and currently losing. I felt my sanity breaking as small sobs broke through and tears mixed with sweat. The slight dampness from the ground soaked into my pants as I knelt numbly in the ruins of the Old Forest. The sky deepened from a bright blue into a rich indigo, spotted pleasantly with distant stars. I laid down on the ground on my back to stare up at the sky, exhaustion soaking into every fiber of my being. I was so tired—mentally and physically. I stayed there, counting the sparkling distant dots as the strong pull of a dream whisked me far away…

My arms and legs screamed in agony as thick metal shackles dug into crusty bleeding sores on my wrists and ankles. The heavy chains were fastened to the stone walls of the dark windowless cell. A weak jangle sounded from the other prisoners as they made the vain attempt to find a comfortable spot to rest.

A pungent rotting odor from human waste mingled with death and moldy hay, making my empty stomach toss and turn angrily. I vacantly wondered how many of these poor souls had already died and the guards had yet to notice, or perhaps they just didn't care. A mouse-like creature scurried along the floors to steal bits of straw and whatever little scraps we were given.

I'd never in my life hoped for death until this moment. The pain in my body joined the pure undiluted terror racing through my mind. My stomach growled painfully loud in hunger as I was reminded of how long I'd been without any real food or drink. I briefly considered eating the skittering rodents for nourishment when the cell door flew open.

I jumped from the sudden noise and shielded my eyes from the light now flooding into the horrid cesspool of a room. As my eyes adjusted to the newfound brightness, I looked around the rectangular chamber. Dozens of bodies laid slumped over in various positions. Their eyes forever frozen in an unseeing gaze. They were long past dead, the mice already taking tiny bites from their cooling flesh.

Tears welled up but didn't fall as I choked back the panic stirring in my chest. I pushed myself into the corner as much as possible, attempting to hide myself behind its former occupant. I peered through my greasy hair strands toward the open doorway.

The light was smothered out by a large shadow as an enormous man stepped into the cell to assess us.

He was easily seven feet tall and packed with muscle. Long dirty blond hair hung past his shoulders, and dark eyes leapt from person to person without emotion. After scanning the room, he turned and spoke to someone behind him. The words were foreign to me as they exchanged them back and forth quickly between each other. The man that was visible nodded his head at the room before exiting.

A slightly smaller man took his place. He carried a long-jumbled pile of chains in his arms. They clattered loudly as he dumped them carelessly onto the filthy stone floor. He grabbed one end and attached it to a metal ring sticking from the wall next to the door. The metal clattered in his hands as he sorted through the pile. The chain of metal links had locks attached to them. He grabbed a lock in one hand and the middle of the nearest person's manacles in the other. He attached the person to the string of metal links, then moved to the next prisoner.

One by one he made his way through the nasty cell to attach the prisoners to this single chain. He checked each body and seemed frustrated to discover how many of them were ultimately dead. He yanked the smelly woman's body away from the corner I took refuge in. He tossed aside her limp corpse without a second glance, then grabbed my manacles to latch onto the string of prisoners. Two others were placed after me.

Once we were all secured, he called out and the larger blond man returned to the cell. He undid the end of the chain and started pulling us out of the rank room. There were ten of us alive, with over a dozen lying dead face down in the straw and human waste. As we were led from the cell mice descended greedily upon the now plentiful source of food.

I was dragged steadily forward. I squeezed my eyes shut as tiny chewing sounds faded away. We shuffled our bare feet across the somewhat warm floor as we walked in silence. The tall man led us up multiple staircases, while the shorter one trailed behind us. My breathing became strained as we neared the top of the twentieth set of stairs. My head spun as a wave of dizziness flooded over me. It took every ounce of strength I had to not pass out on the spot. The others struggled as well, most stumbled, and a few outright fell and were yanked back to their feet.

We slowly marched down a torch-lit hall that was mostly free of any other people. A couple of men and women, also taller than the average person, stared at us as we were paraded in front of them. We halted in front of a massive set of dark doors, they looked to be cherry wood, but my foggy mind wasn't sure how that was possible.

The doors opened into a massive banquet room. The ceilings soared high above us. It was adorned with large chandeliers that danced with glistening crystals. The wall opposite the doors was floor to ceiling windows, though they did little to brighten the dreary room. A table that spanned almost the entire length of the space was covered in what looked like food, though I admit I recognized none of it.

We were pulled to the left of the table where steps led to a small dais containing two ornate throne-like chairs. One was empty, the other filled. We stood in a line facing the seated person. I kept my eyes downcast out of fear but watched from the corner of my eye. The large blond man from the cell was speaking solemnly in the language I didn't understand. One by one he stood behind each prisoner and pulled their head back to look at the seated figure. His steps approached behind me, then his giant hand grabbed a fistful of my hair and pulled, causing me to yelp and my eyes to lift from the dark red carpet into the steely gray eyes of the man perched on the throne-like chair.

I swallowed deeply as his eyes bore into mine intensely. I was speechless as I studied him and he in turn seemed to assess me.

He was an impressively large man, and if I had to venture a guess, I'd say he was taller and more well-muscled than the blond man still clutching my hair in his fist. Long dark hair tumbled down in waves to his upper chest, a strong jaw held pink lips that were formed in a grim line, his nose was crooked, and his eyes were a deep gray, like storm clouds rolling in before a thunderstorm.

I tried to control my breathing as he stared at me. Inside my emotions battled with each other, but I was proud of myself for keeping a stoic exterior. No hint of feeling or emotion passed across his features—they stayed cold. The man behind me finally released his grip on my hair as he moved on to the next person in line. I pulled my eyes back down to the red carpet, it was well worn and dirty were I stood, and I wondered how many others had stood here in rags and chains being judged by the man in the chair.

My morbid thoughts were interrupted by a set of boots that walked into my eyesight. I pulled my eyes up along well-made pants, to a shirt with no arms that displayed every muscle, all the way up to a grim face that towered above me. The man from the chair was looking down at me, my breath caught as he reached out with a large hand and gently gripped my chin. He stroked the pad of his thumb along my jawline, then spoke a few words to someone before he turned and returned to his seat. The greasy blond man hurried over and unlocked me from the long chain that held all the prisoners together, then a stout woman came over to grab my manacles and led me toward the door we had entered though.

I tossed a look over my shoulder, the man in the throne-like chair was watching me as I left the room trailing the woman...

• • •

My eyes snapped open when I slammed back into my body. My heart thundered wildly in my ears as I remembered bits and pieces of the dream. No, not a dream. A memory. A life that was once mine, in a place and time very different to this one. I sucked in a deep steadying breath and took in my surroundings. I was in the Old Forest, still lying in the damp grass, as the sun peeked out above the treetops. Mageia felt so different than it once had, the magic gone long ago. I slowly sat up and movement caught my eye. Panic surged momentarily but was quickly replaced as I realized it was the Ayu. A handful of them were perched at the edge of the tree line, heads tilted ever so slightly to stare at me.

I gave an amused chuckle. "Yes it's me."

They glanced at one another and padded excitedly over to me. What seemed to be the pack leader came close. I held my hand out, and it eagerly sniffed it. It must've accepted my scent as it put its head under my hand and I gently stroked the dark hair of its muzzle. I looked into its eyes and familiarity tugged at me. Not quite recognizing this particular creature but it seemed very similar to the one that took me away from Caleb a long time ago. In a time that was only a few days ago for me but hundreds of years ago for them.

"Exactly how long ago?" I asked the creature. "I don't reckon you could tell me how long it's been since I've been gone?"

It looked at me and tilted its head, giving it a slight shake side to side.

"Yeah, I didn't think so." I dropped my hand solemnly and looked down to the ground that I was lying on. My mind was at a complete loss for what to do next. My heart hurt, it felt shattered and broken. I wanted to be done but I knew I still had so much more to possibly lose.

I glanced once more at the scattered Ayu. "You wouldn't mind taking me back to Azzaria, would you?" It laid down next to me, wagging its tail enthusiastically. "I'll take that as a yes." I scratched its head in appreciation.

I dragged my eyes to the fresh grave before me. I gave a silent goodbye to the man that was once my best friend. A man who deserved so much better than the world gave him and what I was able to give him. I couldn't even give him a proper burial though I knew he probably didn't care either way. If I was able to, one day I'd give him the goodbye he was truly owed, but most of all I would get revenge against those who would take so many innocent people from this world. Those who would kill without conscience, bleeding this land dry, all for a false sense of power.

I gave a quick nod as I said goodbye to Alec and got up from my position on the ground. I climbed on the Ayu, doing my best to hold onto the ginormous beast. I asked it to make haste to Azzaria. I had unfinished business that had been put off for far too long.

Chapter Two

I huffed out a deep breath and groaned heavily, mentally willing myself to open the rusty old door in front of me. I didn't want to, I knew what waited on the other side of it: the vile rancid stench of human excrement mixed with the unmistakable reek of fear and hatred. A sweet cloying scent that choked the nostrils but just under it was a hint of something wrong, a bitterness, or perhaps that was just my wife. Either way the smell made me sick to my stomach daily.

I longed for the days when I could leave and be free to do whatever I pleased, no worries or cares to drag me down. I desired the peaceful moments when I could stand upon the cliffs behind the palace to think, to let the world fall away from me. I missed the feeling of being at the top of the world while the water rose beneath me to crash brutally against the rocky cliff face, the wind whistling past me in a gush of fresh salty ocean air.

I closed my eyes, remembering the faint subtleties of the memory. Something that felt as if it belonged to someone else. It didn't even feel like a memory anymore, just a story that had been told too many times, a bedtime tale that you pretended was real. But it wasn't. What was real was the nightmare we lived in. Being trapped like rats deep under the ground in a place of near darkness. Our eyes and bodies had adjusted slowly over the years to the conditions down here, but not our minds, at least not mine. It still clawed desperately for an escape, for the freedom I once took for granted. What I wouldn't give for just a small taste of it again.

I swallowed hard, for the reality was that I'd never know those feelings and sensations again. The life I once had and enjoyed was long gone. The man I once was had died so long ago I was now a mere figment of him, a fragment of that mind. I was no longer who I was, none of us were. Each of us had changed in such spectacular ways. I thought back often to those days when there was only happiness before everything went so terribly wrong.

I thought about the man who had a bright and promising future, who had a plan to be the best king Azzaria had ever known. What a simple time, for all I knew was forbidden love and stolen moments that I wanted to cherish. There was laughter and a brightness, camaraderie of friends and family. I had a feeling of fulfillment, I desired nothing. Now there was only a dark emptiness and an unending hunger. A never-ending fear, though I admitted to myself it wasn't as strong as it once had been.

Now I was filled with an almost crippling desire for it all to end. I was ashamed of myself for being so weak, but I knew it was a growing want inside of me. I wanted freedom no matter what the cost may be. Funny to think that so long ago, Marcus King of Azzaria only wanted peace and prosperity for his people. Wanted to marry the love of his life, Annabelle, and grow old together. Have beautiful children who would continue our line. That was my future, but it had been ripped away and replaced with an absolute nightmare. I was no longer that man, that strong willful king with hopes and dreams. I was a sad, pathetic, desperate man clinging hopelessly to a life filled with nothing.

The old, rusted door shut squeakily behind me, drawing a bit of attention, but after this many years we no longer jumped at the slightest sound. We all had the feeling of not caring as much, though we still held the fear of being captured by Tatiana and made sure to be cautious. We took up permanent residence under the former whore house that had drawn clientele from all across Tileon, The Swords and Sin.

Its owner, or should I say former owner since Tatiana claimed all businesses as her rightful property, Tyrone still surprisingly kept us company. The greedy little man had grown on me over the years. It wasn't like we had a massive amount of people to talk to down here. We were forced to live with someone whether we liked them or not. So, we tried to find common ground. I couldn't say I loved him or truly liked him, but he was far better company than some were.

I set the brown cloth bag full of small rabbits on the rickety table we used for cooking. Soon my mother, sister, and brother would skin them. They would roast most of them and turn the rest into jerky. We would have food for a little bit, it wasn't much but we did our best. We had gotten more brazen in recent months, sometimes traveling to the edge of the forest to hunt. Not that there was an abundance of food to catch.

Pyron had grown lax in its comfortable position, and

why wouldn't they? They had everything. What did they need to be afraid of? Who was left for Tatiana to be concerned about? There were the remnants of people from Aquaen and Keme who had hoped for sanctuary here, but they quickly joined her cause, bowing easily to her and proclaiming her their rightful new queen.

She sat firmly on the throne in Azzaria, her blood red drakyn always at her side and doing her bidding if a traitor needed to be dealt with. Her brother ruled Pyron in her stead, often traveling here to see her. We overheard Pyron soldiers gossiping that Tatiana preferred the companionship of herself or at times the prisoners she still held beneath the palace. The rumors swirled around viciously, and perhaps we made up a few to make ourselves feel better.

We knew what she desired most of all, and Torrin was far from it. No, she wanted power. And she had it firmly within her grasp. People across Tileon did her bidding, growing food and supplying her army. For her everything was going as she planned.

I felt a bitterness towards it, towards *her*. We could've and should've stopped this. Though a weak, small voice inside my head told me there was absolutely nothing I could have done to prevent the war. I wasn't the person who was meant to stop it, or so Kaia had constantly reminded us. No, that would be my true wife, Niya.

Supposedly she was going to save us all. What a joke, how could a dead woman save us? Kaia held firmly onto the belief that Niya was destined to be our savior but the rest of us knew the sad truth: Tatiana had her killed a long time ago. Along with all the other elementals who opposed her rule.

We scouted the palace often, watching the guards grow

less and less vigilant as the threats to them dwindled down to none. The heads adorning the gate spikes had rotted into mere skulls, the people they once had been were forgotten to time. A new head hadn't been added to Tatiana's collection in at least two months. The elementals had been mostly killed off, only a handful remained, and they were violently loyal to their queen.

I heard the pitter patter of tiny footsteps as a small girl ran up to me, babbling what sounded like dada. I picked her up and gave her a massive squeeze of a hug. She squealed loudly in delight as I placed kisses along her baby face. Pale blonde hair hung to her shoulders, as her gray-green eyes stared up at me in wonder.

"How's my baby girl?" I asked her playfully.

She cooed excitedly as tiny words spilled out in a jumble. I understood a few of them but most came out as gibberish. I held her tightly. Nori had just turned three and my heart broke for her. A filthy foul tunnel was all she and her brother knew as home. I tried to put on a good face for them, but as their father it made my stomach turn to know they would never truly get to enjoy life's pleasures. Never see the sun or walk and play in it as I had, as their mother had.

Instead, they grew up in the stench of shit and other vile things that shouldn't be named. I tried desperately to not dwell on it too much, for when I did it caused an anger to rise in me that was difficult to put away. I held on tightly to a bitterness toward everyone that had been involved in taking away my kingdom, my freedom, my peace.

I set Nori on the floor, and she quickly darted away giggling. I admired her, she found happiness even in one of the darkest of places. I envied her joy, even when I should be thrilled for her. Nori ran to the end of the room where a woman stood with her arms crossed over her chest, her face set in a cold glare.

Perhaps it had been the harsh years, the never-ending fear, lack of food, or just everything combined. But whatever it was, it had been less than kind to her. Anger and bitterness had etched deep lines into her weathered features. Her hair was always matted, and white strands had begun to overrun the blonde ones. Where an easy smile was once often found, now it only held a frown. I couldn't remember the last time I had seen her smile or pretend to be happy. Even towards our children there was a constant rage, maybe it was resentment, a feeling we both shared equally.

My stony demeanor matched hers. Moments of shared love had been stolen from us, anger had chipped away at our marriage as more and more time passed by. As the situation grew longer and we accepted that we were stuck in this place. Hatred bloomed where love had once lived.

I remembered the exact moment it happened. When my love began to fade and a nasty resentment unlike anything I'd felt started to brew deep in my heart. Theo noticed it too but kept his thoughts about it to himself, which I was grateful for. We had found a lost bottle of liquor on one of our outings. We brought it back for everyone to enjoy, unfortunately Annabelle had enjoyed herself a bit too much. Her words had slurred, and she could barely stand as she yelled at every person in the chamber. When she had focused her rage on me, it turned ugly. She loudly voiced her hatred of me, how a better man wouldn't allow his family to rot in such conditions. I kept my mouth shut, not wanting to make the ranting worse, but she threw the bottle at me and it shattered into small glass shards. She screamed at the top of her lungs how deeply she regretted being married to me and how she wished she would've moved on when fate gave her the opportunity to do so. She stormed off to bed muttering how she hoped for my death every time I left the chamber, but so far had the displeasure of my return. After that night, it became well known how much I couldn't stand her presence for very long, a feeling that was mutual.

She blamed me for everything, that we should've given ourselves up years ago and begged for mercy from Tatiana. Given our children the opportunity to live outside of a sewer. I found the whole idea utterly ridiculous. As if Tatiana would give us any fucking grace. The sheer stupidity she had not only here, but that she acted upon during the vote that changed everything for the worse. I had attempted to see things from her point of view, but she acted on impulsive emotion that led to her two small children living under an abandoned whore house.

I wanted to understand it, understand her, but all I could understand was how little she knew. Or perhaps I didn't give her enough credit, maybe she knew that if we surrendered, Tatiana would chop off our heads. At least mine. Annabelle could plead to serve her, saving herself and the children. Maybe her hope was that only my head would end up skewered on top of the gates and she'd be free of me at last. I wanted to ask her if that was her intention, but I felt I already knew the answer.

Her voice came out icy. "That's all you brought back?"

I took a calming breath, trying to keep the simmering rage bottled up inside me at her nasty tone.

"Ten rabbits. To feed all of us?"

"Yes, that's all I was able to catch." My voice came out steady, a feat I'd learned from being a prince.

She glared at me. "I thought there'd be more."

I chuckled, anger coloring it. "You are more than welcome to go out there and hunt them yourself Annabelle if you think you can bring back better. It's not like there's massive amounts of food just out and about. Especially when you're trying to not be killed."

She gave me a disgusted once over and picked up Nori. She turned her back to me, and Nori peeked out over her shoulder waving happily at me. I gave her a faint smile and kept my mouth shut, keeping all the angry words to myself this time.

"You two need to stop. It's not good for the children to see their parents in a state of constant bickering." The voice was on the quiet side, but it didn't need to be loud. The words themselves were like a bucket of ice thrown over me.

I glanced at the corner shrouded in darkness, where my best friend and former advisor sat. Well, at least I thought he was my former advisor, he still thought he needed to give me wise words.

"I'm trying Theo. I'm doing the best I can."

He scoffed. "You could do better, you both could."

I blinked stupidly at him. "What?! What do you want me to do? She blames me when all of this is her fucking mess, her fault. Yet somehow I am to blame for it."

He sighed. "I understand the issues. Trust me, I do. And I'm not saying either one of you is to blame. I'm merely stating that you two being at each other's throat doesn't do anyone any good. It makes things very difficult. You're both on edge, and when people are on edge their minds aren't where they should be."

I ran my hand through my greasy hair that had grown long and messy. "I know. I'm trying. I have tried to make things good with her, but she wants an apology from me. I won't apologize for something that I didn't do wrong. Especially to the person that made the mistake."

"I understand Marcus, I do. I wish there was a magical fix, but there isn't. She hates being trapped down here and I can't blame her one bit for that. I loathe this place as well," he stated sadly.

I looked down at the dirty floor. "She wants us to surrender. She thinks that in all these years, Tatiana's heart has softened and that she'll keep us under lock and key with guards in the palace. Take the children as her wards, which would be a better life than here. You know that would never happen. I know that the first thing Tatiana would do would be to sever our heads from our bodies. Yours, mine, Landen's, perhaps Tyrone's for giving us shelter. We would all end up with our heads on spikes. For all we know, she'd feed my children to her drakyn. She can't allow anyone with royal blood to roam free. Yet Annabelle has her head stuck in the clouds with wild hopes and dreams."

The older man looked grim. "You're probably right. Chances are that Tatiana is more paranoid now than ever. While we hear the random rumor here and there, it's been a long time since anyone's been even remotely able to challenge her." He walked over slowly and put his hand on my shoulder. A sign of camaraderie but also a sign he had also given up hope.

"It'll be okay. Can't go on forever, right?" I gave him a sad smile.

I heard a buzz of voices stirring as everyone gathered in the common room. There was a grateful excitement about the rabbits I had caught, and I was glad they at least appreciated my efforts. Fresh food was a huge deal for us, helping us keep whatever strength we had. I watched them start to prep the rabbits for cooking when I noticed something odd. Kaia looked different today. There was an excited bounce in her step and in the way she carried herself. Though the thought was whisked away when Landen pulled my attention to him.

He looked over my catch. "How was it out there?"

"Same as usual. Few guards here and there. A couple patrolled the outer edges of the forest. For the most part it didn't seem like they were interested in the rabbits. I noticed more rabbits were venturing closer to the edge of the Azzarian forest. Also saw a few birds fluttering around."

"The more food the better, that's what I say!" Tyrone said with a laugh as he prepared some drinking water. The once rotund man had lost a lot of weight. He had been a gluttonous little thing, eating all kinds of exotic meats, cheeses, and other rare delicacies from across Tileon. Now he was lucky to get half a rabbit once a week.

Landen gave a laugh. "Yes, food is always a good thing."

I was about to make a joke about the meager amount of food when a distant sound came from the end of one of the tunnels. My heart leapt into my throat as everyone instantly stopped what they were saying and doing. I heard knives clatter to the ground as we stood there like statues, frozen in fear.

There were three offshoots of tunnels running under the Swords and Sin. Two large tunnels that we lived in and one smaller one. From my understanding of what Tyrone had told us, the tunnels moved the waste from this building out to the river. The smaller tunnel had steel grates at the end, and it was supposed to be extremely difficult to find the opening as it was down deep into the riverbank.

Yet a loud clatter was coming from that direction. It halted the breath in my throat. I didn't dare breathe or move a muscle. My mind screamed at me to grab my sword, but my body wouldn't move. No one did. My heart thundered louder and louder. Or was that the sound of footsteps? Yes, footsteps grew in volume as a paralyzing fear consumed me completely. Pyron finally found us.

Oh fuck. All I could think about was my children and what would happen to them. A nasty dark part of my mind hoped whatever was done to them was after my certain death. I couldn't bear the thought of watching them in pain. My breath was raspy, coming out in ragged shallow puffs. I wanted to throw up, but I swallowed down the bile.

My eyes went wide, desperately searching the darkness of the tunnel. For the glimmer of armor and steel. How many? How many did she send to take us? Would they kill us here and leave our bodies to rot? Or would she publicly execute us? The thoughts raced wildly through my mind. I could barely follow them as they jumped from one horrible thing to the next.

Finally, the owner of the footsteps came into view. Confusion knitted my brows together. It was a single person dressed head to toe in black. Strange armor adorned their body and I realized they were a lot smaller than I expected them to be. Though I suppose that made sense if they squeezed through the grates.

They pulled back their head covering that was wrapped securely around their head and face. Shock washed over me as recognition hit. From behind me, Tyrone's bewildered voice sounded out like a trumpet in the silent room. I knew it was more of a whisper, but it sounded so much louder to my ears.

"Niya?"

The beautiful woman grinned. "Wow, y'all look like shit."

Chapter Three

I stood there dumbfounded, blinking my eyes rapidly. They wanted desperately to process what they were seeing. My brain was frantically trying to catch up to my mouth to say something, anything, but words wouldn't come out. The others stood there mumbling quietly as they took in the person standing before us.

Finally, Tyrone broke the near silence as I heard him take a few steps forward and repeated the name. "Niya?"

She raised an eyebrow, just staring at the man. "Yeah, that would be me."

"H-How?" he stuttered. She gazed at him confused. "H-H-How are you alive?"

A dark look crossed over her features. "That's a long story and not one I wish to tell right now. But thanks for the vote of confidence."

"It's just been so long since anyone saw you," Tyrone replied.

"I guess." She shrugged. "A few months can feel like a long time I suppose."

I glanced over to the man who once owned this woman. He seemed bewildered.

Theo interjected, "It hasn't been a few months my lady."

"What are you talking about?" Her eyes moved from face to face. "Okay so maybe it was more than a couple of months, maybe a year. My time is a little off at the moment." She gave a little chuckle as if telling a joke.

I gave Theo a glance, and finally words came out of my mouth. "It's been much longer than a year Niya. The last time we saw you at the palace, before you left, was over five years ago."

Her face fell as her eyes widened. She straightened her back and adjusted her armor, shifting uncomfortably. "Excuse me?"

"It's been five years since we saw you. The night you left was a long time ago. It was before..."

"Before...what?" she asked loudly, eyes darting between all of us.

I glanced around awkwardly. "Before the war started."

She shook her head. "No. That can't be. I've only been gone..." Her words drifted off into silence, and she stared at the floor, eyes going back and forth as though she was lost in thought. Her eyebrows knitted together, and she took a deep annoyed breath before looking back at us. "Oh. I thought it had been less time."

I asked the question I assumed was on everyone's mind. "Where have you been all these years? Surely not hiding in the forest." I took in her appearance and a slight twinge of jealousy spiked in me. She was clean and seemed to be well fed, with not a scratch on her. The armor she wore was in pristine condition—unlike us living in a shit filled sewer wearing nothing more than rags and whatever else we could scrounge together. We had all lost weight, choosing to give most of the food we were able to attain to the children while we fell into starvation, desperation, and eventual hopelessness. She seemed to have not had the same horrible five years as we did.

She bit her lip. "I was where I needed to be."

"What is that supposed to mean?" I asked with a slight edge to my voice.

Her eyes narrowed to slits. "It means that's all you need to know, Marcus. I wasn't coming here for a fucking interrogation."

"Why did you come here then? How did you know we were even here?" My suspicions started to rise as it struck me that she could be working for Tatiana.

She glared at me coldly. It was evident in her eyes how stupid the question was to her. "I didn't know you were going to be here. As a matter of fact, I was told you were all dead. So why did you come down here? I understand it's been five years since we last saw each other, but you forget where you found me. Here at this place, this establishment," she said it in a sarcastic, chiding manner. I definitely felt stupid. "I was raised here, grew up within these walls. This is my home. You think I wouldn't know how to get in and out of here undetected? I came here because I didn't know where else to go and wanted a familiar place to sleep. I had no idea I would find anyone or anything here."

Tyrone stepped a few feet closer to her. "I didn't think I would ever see you again." He glanced behind her in search of something. "Where's Alec?"

Her face darkened but her eyes didn't leave Tyrone's as

she whispered, "He didn't make the journey." Her voice was filled with sorrow.

For the first time since I'd known the man, Tyrone looked physically shaken. His mouth quivered as tears gathered in his eyes. He was barely able to choke out, "When?"

"Not long after we left, maybe a few months."

Tyrone sniffled. "H-H-How did he..." He couldn't finish the sentence.

She knew what he was asking. "He was shot in the throat by a Pyronian archer. It was quick." The balding man shook his head and tears fell freely from his face. "I'm sorry Tyrone, I didn't think I'd be the one handing you such news. I honestly didn't think I'd see any of you again, especially not like this." She glanced around at everyone's stunned faces.

A small quiet settled over the group and a tiny noise drew our attention away from our new guest. The little steps of a child made pitter patter sounds as Annabelle and the children came out of their hiding spot. Nori walked in front of her as Riley stood behind her. Annabelle took one long look at Niya, studying her every inch. Her lips formed a tight line, and she leveled a glare in my direction. Her eyes moved back to the other woman, and she bowed her head slightly. "I see our queen has returned."

Niya's eyes widened. "Hardly. Since she never left." She looked at Annabelle pointedly, then down to the children. "And the queen has a little prince and very cute princess."

Niya gave Nori a warm smile, one that was well received by my little girl, but Annabelle did not accept the compliment. "I'm hardly royalty, as we are all very well aware. Perhaps if you had been here in my place, you wouldn't have made the same mistake as I did."

Niya crossed her arms. "I'm afraid I don't understand what you're referring to. But quite frankly, I'm not interested in any domestic squabbles. If there's something you need to speak to Marcus alone about, you are more than welcome to do so but I won't be dragged into the middle of it." Niya gave her a firm look and Annabelle nodded weakly, but her face made her feelings clear, she was not pleased to see Azzaria's true queen here.

"Come children, let's go." Annabelle escorted them briskly back down the tunnel, practically dragging Nori with her. The small girl giggled and waved to our newcomer, who waved back.

A small voice piped up with a chuckle, "Well, that was awkward, wasn't it?"

I glanced at Landen, giving the man a dark look. "Obviously."

Landen gave Niya a once over and smiled broadly at her. "Marcus, you did not tell me that Niya was such a delightful presence."

She grinned wickedly at the older man. "He doesn't think I'm a delight."

"Well, you certainly are. You, my dear, may call me Landen." He stuck a hand out to her, and she gave it a quick shake. "My, what a grip."

Niya scoffed. "Fascinating. So, tell me about the last five years. What did I miss?"

I'm not a fan of surprises. In my experience they usually don't turn out pleasantly, and there always seems to be a hidden catch.

I had snuck into the bowels of Azzaria to make my way towards my old home. A familiar place to lay my head and rest felt like a welcome change of pace. I knew something was amiss when I entered the tunnel. The smell wasn't as atrocious as it normally was, and the slight echo of voices traveled along the slimy brick walls.

My heart dropped for a moment as I thought soldiers had taken up residence inside the former whore house. Or perhaps the women I grew up with were still trapped here in dire conditions. My mind created so many horrible imaginary scenarios, I couldn't think straight.

Until I heard the voices more clearly and I knew they were somehow familiar to me. But the people they belonged to were supposed to be dead, or so the scouts in Heka assumed. I swallowed back any uncertainty I had, not sure how it would be to see them again, but I'd come too far to turn back now.

I placed one foot in front of the other and stepped into the chamber that connected all the tunnels to one another. And there in the middle, with panicked terror etched on their faces, stood the last people I expected to see down here. It was amusing, however, to see their faces when they realized it was me. They needed a long moment to process my presence and I was grateful for it. I needed time to process the sight in front of me too.

There were about a dozen people give or take in the grimy chamber. From the looks of it, they had been living here for a while. They had a makeshift kitchen in one corner and a seating area in another. I glanced at the openings of the other two tunnels, dirty blankets with holes in them hung down to create a false sense of privacy in the sewage room. I assumed they used those tunnels for sleeping accommodations since the stench radiating from them hadn't been as severe as the main tunnel.

The two men in the front of the group looked worn down and filthy but I still recognized the advisor and king for who they were. Then my eyes met dark brown ones and my breath caught in my throat. Tyrone was alive and living with the royal family. He wasn't dead. I don't know why this discovery came as a surprise to me, of course his weasel ass would find a way to survive when better men were dead.

I didn't recognize the others in the room, there was a faint familiarity, but everyone was in such incredibly rough shape it was hard to tell. I vaguely noticed the conversation at hand, my body and voice were present, but my mind was far away. It was grasping at anything and everything except for the truth right in front of me.

Five years...five fucking years. I'd ask myself how, but I already knew the answer.

Azzaria and Tileon had been under Tatiana's rule for over five years, and I'd been gone for most of it. How much destruction had she caused that I could've been here to prevent? How many lives had been lost that I could've saved? I tried not to be angry at something that was outside of my control, but I still felt guilty that I hadn't been here when I was needed most.

Maybe the guilt was also tied to now having to tell Tyrone how I failed. Alec left here to be with me, and I took him from Heka's safety back into this world. He died because of me, my selfishness. One of the most powerful Vayu to live and I couldn't save one life. What's the point of power if you can't save the ones you love?

I left Caleb behind like a coward, left him to a life with a woman he hadn't wanted. I couldn't even give him the respect to tell him to his face. No instead I'd snuck away in the middle of the night like a thief with only a note to explain myself. I was a selfish coward who was supposed to save an entire world. How could I do that when I couldn't even help the two people I loved the most?

My attention drifted from my self-loathing toward the people surrounding me. I hated that they held wonder and awe on their faces while they all stared at me. I wasn't the person they wanted me to be, but I wasn't going to cruelly step on their hopes and dreams.

"Can't say you missed much," Marcus stated.

I glanced around then raised my eyebrow. "Seems like I missed a lot. You have children and live in the sewer under my old home."

He looked down, not daring to meet my eyes. "Annabelle was in her early pregnancy when Azzaria… surrendered to Tatiana. We had hoped she'd show mercy but she's devoid of such compassion. Landen helped us escape the palace alive, while Theo brought us here. It was meant to be temporary living quarters, but it became clear after a while that there was nowhere else to go."

"You thought a woman that murdered her own father and massacred an entire nation would be merciful?" I asked incredulously.

His gray-blue eyes flickered up to mine. "Some of us felt that way, not all."

I scoffed. "Hmph, you're lucky you made it out alive."

"I'm well aware."

Theo interrupted our discussion. "What happened can't be undone, we can only fix what is currently broken." He looked at me with hope filled eyes. "You have returned to help us, correct?"

I nodded bleakly. "I'm going to try my best." The sentiment was true, but my confidence was far from optimistic. I hadn't prepared myself to handle that anyone I knew was still alive, that I still had something to lose to Tatiana if I failed. But Alec once told me to fake it until I made it a reality. If I pretended it to be true, eventually it would be, right?

They all grinned at the news. The man who called himself Landen was a curious individual, he portrayed himself in such an unserious manner. But under the surface there was a cunningness hiding there. He studied me in a knowing way that set my nerves on edge. He was younger than Theo but had white hints of age weaving throughout his black hair. His eyes were a glacier blue that didn't seem to miss much, and he stood taller than anyone else by at least six inches. He smiled broadly when he saw me watching him. "If I might be so bold to ask, how do you plan on helping us out of our current predicament?"

Everyone looked at me with wide eyes, waiting for a clever plot to overthrow Pyron. I cleared my throat. "Well…I haven't exactly thought that far ahead. I wasn't fully ready for this situation. Right now, my only plan is to kill Tatiana and go from there."

Landen pursed his lips. "That's a solid start. But others would seek revenge for their lost queen. We need a plan to root out and get rid of all the rotten parts of Pyron."

"You're talking about a full-on war?"

He shrugged. "If that's what it takes. You've been gone a long time. Those years have been filled with the blood of the innocent, their deaths. Whether those soldiers or people responsible started off with clean hands doesn't matter anymore. Their hands are dirty now, they've obeyed vile orders without question and done unspeakable deeds in Tatiana's name. I don't doubt your intentions, but I don't think even you can erase all that wickedness by killing one woman."

"I don't know, yet. I'm not willing to sacrifice countless more lives without a shred of knowledge and a solid plan in place first. I'm not itching for a war, are you?" I asked coldly.

He chuckled darkly. "She nearly wiped out all of my people. Perhaps she did. Only a few hundred out of thousands had survived and sought out Azzaria for refuge before Tatiana took the throne. I can only guess at the horrific fate she gave them." I looked at him, confused. "I don't expect you to know me. I was the king of Aquaen. So yes, I'm itching for a fight, have been for many years."

"I'm sorry for your loss, I can only imagine. I saw the destruction distantly and that was unspeakably disgusting to witness. But I'm not here to settle scores. I won't slaughter all of Pyron just so you feel like their debt to you is now paid. I want to avoid any more mass killings. I won't be like her."

He stared at me with evident pity. "We don't always get what we wish for. Sometimes we must prepare ourselves for the inevitable."

"We will try it your way, Niya. But we should prepare for any other unfortunate outcomes," Theo said, breaking up mine and Landen's talk of what he felt like was an unavoidable war.

I was grateful for the interruption. "Where is Tatiana currently?"

They looked at one another, shrugging.

Marcus answered my question. "We can't know for

absolute certain, but we haven't seen her leave beyond the gates in years. Her drakyn patrols the sky above Azzaria daily while she holes up in the comfort of the palace. She used to actively offer a reward for elementals, or the mystery woman in the Old Forest that killed her men." He looked pointedly at me. "But they obviously never found you. As for the elementals…they found all of the ones they could. Their heads adorn the gates. After a while Tatiana gave up the search. She holds Tileon firmly in her control. Why bother with weak people that couldn't oppose her if they tried?"

I closed my eyes as my stomach churned. Elementals killed for no reason. My guilt grew. I could've trained them, saved them from their fate. "Is Tatiana in the palace alone?"

Theo scoffed. "Hardly. Guards patrol the gates and outer gardens frequently. We don't know how many she has in other areas of the palace grounds, or inside the palace itself. Only the most loyal are allowed inside the gates. The rest of her forces sweep the city constantly."

I rubbed my fingers along my forehead in annoyance. I had hoped Tatiana had grown lazy after so many years, but instead she was well protected and secure. "How do you leave here? You have fresh meat. You must have a way around the city that's somewhat safe."

"I wouldn't say it's safe but it's the least watched route and worth the risk for food," Marcus said hesitantly.

"Show me."

The men blinked, taken aback by the demand. Marcus stuttered, "Y-you want to go out there? We just went out for this week's supplies, maybe in a few days we can take you out."

I crossed my arms; my face took on a hardness. "It

wasn't a question. I want to see the city now, with or without your help."

Theo sighed, time had worn him down and he didn't want to argue when he knew it was a lost cause. "Very well but stay close. We can't afford to lose you after we just got you back."

I nodded. "I will. Show me how bad things have gotten."

Chapter Four

I was ready to leave immediately. Marcus and Theo, however, were less than thrilled to be departing from the relative safety of the sewage tunnels, but they weren't willing to let me go alone. They took a few minutes to pack up a couple items before saying their "I'll be back soon's". During their packing I was introduced to the others who resided in the rank chamber. I already knew Tyrone, Marcus, Theo, and now Landen, and I quickly met Marcus's mother Lady Trina, his brother Zander, and youngest sister Elissa.

I was somewhat embarrassed that I was meeting his family this way. They hadn't been able to attend our rushed wedding ceremony since they were with the former king when he passed. I tried to give them as warm of a smile as I could plaster on my face. While I was happy to finally meet them, I was anxious to leave. I was told that the small little girl was Nori, and the young boy was Riley, I didn't get an opportunity to say anything to them—Annabelle kept them out of sight.

The last person I was introduced to was one of

Landen's daughters Kaia. She was the friendliest of the bunch as she wrapped her arms around me and squeezed tightly. Her features were bright and cheery, which was the opposite of how the others looked. She took after her father, a seemingly unserious exterior that disguised a very clever mind. I watched her closely, there was something about her I couldn't quite put my finger on. If I didn't know better, I'd say she carried a hidden burden, but I wasn't going to ask her directly about such musings.

I was itching to depart; I wasn't in the mood to entertain all the glances and questions I was receiving. Everyone seemed okay with Marcus and Theo escorting me around the city except Annabelle, who glared relentlessly in our direction. I was confused by her obvious distaste for her husband let alone myself. I had only met her briefly when we switched places, and she came off as such a sweet and kind person then. I couldn't help but wonder what changed to make her so cold and distant.

We finally took our leave of the tunnel system, waving a halfhearted goodbye. The old rusty metal door squeaked open, and the two men clenched their jaws tightly at the sound and looked around wildly in the next room for any signs of soldiers. While I understood the intense paranoia, their jumpiness was alarming. I shut the door behind me with a solid thud and moved on.

It was strange to see the Swords and Sin in this manner, I'd never seen it empty let alone in a state of such disrepair and decay. The floors were coated in dirt, while cobwebs dangled randomly from the ceiling. Dust floated through the stale air and held a musty odor.

I whispered to Theo a question that had been on my mind since my return. "What happened to everyone that lived here?"

He turned around halfway to answer me. "I'm not fully sure. When we came here Tyrone was already alone, he has never talked about any others or what became of their fates. Many in the city fled to who knows where. Those that stayed behind are few and far between."

I nodded grimly and continued to follow a few steps behind the men. I quickly glanced up the abandoned stairs in the main entry. My room was up there, along with dozens of other girls'. I didn't dare dwell on what possibly happened to them. I wasn't ready yet to do so.

We carefully snuck out of the back of the building into the alleyway, listening closely to the noises around us. We didn't hear any footsteps beyond our own, or the clanking of armor. Keeping close to the brick walls and letting the shadows cloak us, I was shown the absolutely devastating wreck that had once been a thriving city in Tileon.

The gray cobblestones of the street were currently coated in a filthy brown-red color. The stains ran like old crimson rivers, some areas darker than others. A tangy copper scent filled my nostrils as I realized the streets were caked with excessive amounts of dried blood. I swallowed my disgust as we moved deeper into the city towards the market square and palace grounds.

We passed countless homes that were in a similar state to the Swords and Sin. Dark red handprints and splatters covered the walls inside. What windows were intact had a grimy film and plants grew out of cracks. Doors hung haphazardly on ungreased hinges, desperately clinging to their former glory. Uneaten animal food lay rotten and forgotten in bowls, their owners' small bones discarded nearby. Flies buzzed around random piles of who knew what in a joyous dance; the winged insects had been well fed. Vultures circled the gray sky greedily, waiting for their next opportunity at a fresh carcass.

My eyes watered from either the wretched state of this familiar area or the foul stench that permeated everything. I'd soon discover this wasn't even the worst of it. No, that honor went to the palace—or what remained of it.

The once gleaming golden gates were no longer sparkling decorations, they were now a gory warning. The gold metal was not visible at this distance, just a solid dark red. Pieces of flesh stuck here and there to the bars. The source of them rested upon thick spikes at the top of the gates. Hundreds of heads in various states of decomposition spanned the whole row of metal fencing. Skulls with jaws detached sat next to faces freshly deceased, their eyes not yet glazed over. At the base, strewn along the outside walkway, were piles of bodies and other dead things.

My mouth fell open at the grisly scene. How many hundreds of Azzarian people were now crudely displayed on top of the palace gates? Everywhere my eyes darted I saw only death and suffering. The whole outer courtyard was no longer fresh green grass, but burnt dirt mixed with flesh to mark a drakyn's nest. My breath became ragged as rage boiled up inside me.

"The beheadings don't occur nearly as much as they once did. Only a handful are added every year now," Marcus said softly.

I wasn't sure if it was a weak attempt at comforting me, but his words didn't calm the anger I felt. "None should be added at all. Where do they come from?"

Theo shrugged. "No one knows exactly. They aren't Azzarian as far as I recognize them. But it's difficult to know for sure."

"Rumor is that they are strays she keeps locked in the

dungeons. She displays them every so often to remind people who's in charge and to behave," Marcus added.

I didn't utter a single word, my eyes still glued morbidly on the gruesome display of power.

"We should go back. We've been out here long enough," Marcus stated warily. I nodded grimly, prying my eyes away from the bloody mess.

We turned to leave when a sudden commotion drew our attention. Loud voices echoed around the empty market square. I ducked behind a brick wall and peeked out towards the gates. There were two soldiers dragging a frightened woman between them by her upper arms. She was kicking and screaming. The soldiers took her to the entrance of the gate, where four others stood watching the theatrical display.

I looked around to make sure we were still mostly alone before sneaking closer to the chaotic scene. I vaguely heard Theo and Marcus's panicked whispers telling me to come back. I had tuned them out to focus solely on the woman. I was close enough to hear her frantic pleas as she begged them to stop.

"Please, I didn't do anything I swear!" she sobbed.

One of the soldiers backhanded her hard on the cheek. "Quiet. We know you're a liar and a traitor."

"No, I'm not! I'm loyal to the queen, truly!"

"Then why did we catch you stealing food from her majesty's supply caravan?"

"I-I didn't know it was hers. I swear I didn't." She wailed pitifully.

The soldier got closer to her face. "So, you admit you're a thief."

The woman cried louder. "I-I-I have a family. My children are hungry. I was only going to take a small amount. Please sir, I didn't mean any harm."

The soldier glanced at the two still firmly holding her, their meaty paws digging painfully into her flesh. "Hear that? She's just stealing from our beloved queen to feed her useless brats."

The other soldiers laughed at her. Her sobs grew in volume. "Please…please. I won't do it again. Please!"

The soldier freed his sword from the scabbard. "Damn right you won't. Hold her."

She screamed out. "HELP PLEASE! SOMEONE HELP ME!"

My wrist started to burn, the magic waking up to answer her call. I didn't give it a second's thought. Didn't dare look back to Theo and Marcus. I just stood up and abandoned my hiding spot within the shadows and stepped out into the light.

I grabbed a small knife from my thigh pouch and threw it with all my strength. A wet squish was the only sound as it embedded itself into the soldier's forehead. His eyes went wide, and he fell back with a solid thud. The remaining soldiers whipped their heads towards me.

I stood about ten feet away and said firmly, "Release her."

The soldiers looked at one another, one spoke up. "Kill her now!"

"Hard way it is then," I mumbled to myself. I took my dual swords from their place upon my back armor and gripped them tightly in my hands.

The two soldiers who held the woman continued to do so, though they looked at me nervously. The other three fumbled to get their swords out and at the ready. They walked past the captive woman to make a semi-circle around me. The one in the middle attacked first, rushing in and swinging his sword wildly. I pushed him into the soldier on my left, their swords and bodies tangled together as I made my move on the soldier to the right.

He brought down his sword, but I used mine to block him. I flicked his sword away from me and plunged my right blade deep into his gut with a satisfying twist. He crashed to the ground just as the other two regained their wits.

They circled me slowly. As one went into my blind spot he stabbed at me, his blade sliding across my side. I squeezed my arm down, pinning the sword in place. I kicked out hard behind me and connected with one of their knees. I heard multiple cracks as their knee shattered and now faced the wrong direction. They let out a pained shriek as they fell to the ground in agony. The last soldier mistakenly glanced at their now hobbled friend, giving me the opportunity to slash my sword's edge cleanly across his exposed throat. Bright crimson red poured out of the gash to join the dried blood already on the cobblestone street. I turned around and plunged one of my swords into the hobbled soldier's chest. The magically made metal slid in easily as the life left his body.

The two remaining soldiers stood frozen as the woman hung between them with a stunned expression on her face. Finally, one of them let go of her arm to grab a dagger from his belt. He threw it weakly, and it landed in my arm. I stared at the hilt and sighed heavily, then glanced back at him. I pulled the dagger out with a pained grunt. The soldier who threw it looked terrified, and he turned around to run to the entrance of the gate. I chucked the bloody dagger and it landed between his shoulder blades. He fell face first into the pile of discarded bodies.

The last living soldier stared wide eyed at the body then back at me. They gulped, dropped the woman's arm, and made a dash for the gates. I strode purposefully towards them, putting my dual blades away. The soldier pounded frantically on the metal bars and screamed loudly for help. But no one was going to come, they were too used to the pleas to take notice. I passed by the woman who knelt on the walkway rubbing her upper arms and bent down to retrieve my knife from the first soldier's forehead. I walked over to the last soldier who was still screaming at the top of their lungs for help and beating wildly on the gates. I stood next to them calmly as they turned to look at me. Tears filled their eyes and rolled down their cheeks. The smell of piss drifted up to my nose.

"Please…I have a family."

I narrowed my eyes. "So does she." I stabbed the knife hilt deep into their throat, silencing their useless pleas forever.

I looked back to the woman. She looked at me with concern. "Are you okay?" she asked quietly.

"I should be asking you that," I replied.

"I—Thank you."

I nodded briskly, slightly uncomfortable. I was not good at helping people or accepting their gratitude. "It was nothing. But you need to leave now. Take your kids away from the city."

She looked unsure then got up and ran from the bloody city square. I didn't blame her, I was tempted to do the same, but a foolish idea sprang into my mind and took root there. I could do it now, make my way into the palace and kill Tatiana. Deal with the inevitable fall out later. The gates were ajar, what better chance would I get? I sighed and entered the gates.

I walked along a gravel and dirt road that led to the top of the hill that had been flattened to make the palace grounds. My footsteps were steady as I trekked up the path. As I reached the top and could fully see the palace, guards spotted me.

"Hey! Halt!" I stopped and watched, amused as a dozen armed guards came running. "Put your weapons on the ground now!"

I gave them a wicked grin, letting my power ooze out around me. My hands now had purple flames coming from them. The guards took a few steps back.

I raised my eyebrow. "How about you take me to see the queen?"

Chapter Five

The guards promptly escorted me inside the palace to see Tatiana. I was amused that they gave me a wide berth, keeping their distance and not even bothering to remove my weapons. What would be the point to take away a couple of swords and some daggers, when that same woman could spew purple flames from her hands?

I wasn't sure what I expected the interior of the palace to look like, especially after seeing the grizzly bloody mess outside, but I prepared myself for more of the same rotten shit. However, I was met with an unexpected sight. The inside was surprisingly devoid of blood, flesh, and decaying corpses.

The walls were painted a deep, dark rich red mixed with hints of black. The airy feeling of the hallways had been replaced with a dark cramped smothered feeling. It reminded me vividly of the capitol of Pyron, Fajro. I wondered if that had been the inspiration for the decor decisions. The art had been replaced as well, the new pieces reflecting the new queen's ideals. Statues and numerous paintings depicted different drakyns ripping people apart, the land of Pyron in all its glory, Fajro's black palace, and a truly incredible number of images of what I assumed were of Tatiana.

I was led directly to the throne room, which was an extremely large chamber that I had previously explored during my short time here. It had intricately carved wooden doors that told of Azzaria's history, Caleb's history. The two massive doors opened into a bright sunny room, the thrones for the king and queen rested on a dais straight across from the entrance. Along the back wall were floor to ceiling glass windows that overlooked the gardens and had a great view of the ocean.

At least that's how the room once looked. The centuries' old specially made doors were gone, their hinges still hanging from the door frame. I was incredibly shocked that Tatiana hadn't replaced them with new doors that depicted her reign. The two thrones of pale blue stone were no longer there, in their place was one single enormous throne made entirely of pitch-black stone. My mind flashed back to my time in the black palace in front of a similar looking throne. This chamber now held a sense of malice in its air, putting my nerves on edge. I steadied myself. I had gotten rid of one Pyron tyrant, a second one should be easy.

I stopped in the middle of the room. The guards retreated from the chamber to stand in the hall. The sound of a small side door opening echoed loudly, and my eyes flicked to the left where the noise came from.

A tall woman gracefully strode in. Her raven black hair was tightly pulled back into a sleek ponytail, showcasing her angular features. She wore a blood red top with black pants. Her eyes were a dark void with a fiery orange around the edges and they studied me closely. She stood for a minute at the base of the dais silently watching. Then who I assumed was Tatiana walked to the throne and sat down, but not fully. She stayed towards the edge of the seat and sat stiffly.

I didn't say anything, no, I wanted her to speak first. I stood with a bored expression plastered on my face. She tapped the tips of her fingers along the armrest of the stone throne. After a few minutes of tense silence, she finally broke out in a sly grin.

"You asked for me," she stated in a bored tone.

"I wouldn't say I asked," I replied.

Her grin held something beneath it, but I hadn't put my finger on it yet. "No. You demanded. After killing six of my soldiers."

I shrugged nonchalantly. "They deserved it."

She tilted her head ever so slightly. "Hmm. May I ask why?"

I'll admit, I slipped up for a moment and looked confused. "They were going to kill an innocent woman."

"How noble of you to save her. It's been a while since anyone has risked their life for a stranger."

I stared at her. "I didn't feel like it was any risk to me to help."

Her eyebrows went up in mock surprise. "Is that so?"

I smirked confidently. "It is."

Her grin grew feline. "Perhaps it wasn't a risk for you. However..." She motioned with her hand to the guards. I turned my head as two guards brought in a bound and gagged woman. Blood trickled slowly from a cut on her temple to drip down her face. My eyes widened and my breath caught in my throat, it was the woman I had saved by the gates. They took her over to the foot of the dais. She locked eyes with mine, hers filled with pure terror.

The queen sat perched quietly before nodding to one of the guards. He drew a blade and held it close to the exposed neck of the frightened woman. Tears streamed down her cheeks as she closed her eyes tightly. "It seems it was a huge risk to her," Tatiana stated coldly.

I swallowed my rising panic, my heart thundering wildly in my chest. I wasn't prepared for this turn of events. I had assumed the woman had escaped the city. "She's not a part of this."

"But she is. She was to receive the queen's justice and you prevented that. How would it look to have someone escape punishment? Others would attempt to follow, and chaos would ensue. Ruling is quite simple. Someone breaks the rules and they in turn get punished."

I glared at her angrily. "Since when is the punishment death? Sounds more like you enjoy hurting people and this has given you the opportunity to do so freely without question."

She shrugged casually. "All crimes are subject to the death penalty. I find it keeps one's subjects…in line."

I curled my lip in disgust. "That's not ruling. You're killing Tileon, murdering its people, just to feel powerful?"

Her lips pursed. "Power is subjective, isn't it? I hold all of Tileon in my hands. Power like that isn't given, it's taken with brute force. The strong survive and thrive while the weak wither and die. It's nature. Should I share some of that power with you?"

I shook my head vehemently. "I don't want it. That's not my idea of ruling or power."

Her eyes narrowed. "It wasn't a choice. You now hold this woman's life in your hands. Let's be completely honest with one another, shall we? You answer my questions truthfully and she lives, agreed?"

I swallowed hard, staring at the silently sobbing woman still held tightly by the guards. I looked at Tatiana and nodded once.

Her grin returned and her dark eyes glistened. She was enjoying this game. "Good. You're very interesting. It's been so long since anyone dared to question me so boldly. You're used to being in charge."

It was said as a statement, but I answered it as if she asked, trying to be somewhat honest. "Actually no."

Her eyebrow rose in true surprise. "I said to be truthful," she chastised.

"I am. I didn't grow up wealthy or with anything to my name. In fact, it was the opposite, all I had was my name."

"And your unique gifts?"

I wasn't sure why the question made me nervous, but my palms began to sweat. I couldn't underestimate her or how much intel she had on me. "I didn't have them for most of my life." In that moment, I saw no harm in telling her, either way I held the power here. I could kill her whenever I wanted to. Right?

She mulled over my words. "Then they are newer to you. And you seemed to have such a strong opinion on ruling." She tilted her head again, studying me.

"Is that a question or just your opinion?"

Her smile widened. "Just my observation. The observation of an interesting woman with abilities I haven't seen before, that seems to be a great fighter. Years ago, there were rumors of such a woman. She was a royal by all accounts and became queen here in Azzaria."

My heart sank into a pit in my stomach. I kept my mouth firmly closed.

She laughed coldly at my silence. "I believe that woman's name was…it's on the tip of my tongue. Ah yes, it was Niya."

My blood turned to ice; I hadn't expected her to know who I was.

"I'm going to take your silence to mean I'm indeed correct. That is you, is it not?"

"It is. I am Niya, queen of Azzaria and princess of Mageia."

Her face turned stony, all hints of smugness gone. "Former queen. Your husband and his…mistress surrendered to me. I am queen of Tileon."

I locked my eyes on hers, not giving any indication of the terror I felt. "As you stated, my husband and his mistress made that decision. I, the true queen, would never surrender to you. Nor have I."

"Azzaria is mine, whether you gave it to me or that other woman did. In the end it makes no difference. This is my throne, my kingdom, and my lands," she spat.

"For now."

Barely concealed rage flickered across her features, and her teeth gritted together. "I see that you haven't learned your place yet." She motioned to the guard still holding the blade to the woman's neck. He quickly slid the sharp edge across the exposed skin of her throat. Blood immediately poured out like a waterfall of red. The woman's eyes lost the life in them as she crumpled to the ground.

I watched helplessly as the warm pool of crimson spread out on the floor. She was lying on her stomach, her face turned in my direction. Her eyes stared at me, the look of terror still etched on her face. I had saved her for only a brief moment. She ended up dead anyway.

"I hope you understand your place now. You aren't anyone's savior or queen. Let this be a good lesson to you." She said the words proudly. She took a woman's life…to teach me a lesson.

I stared at the forever stilled body on the floor. Then drew my gaze to the figure sitting proudly on the black stone throne. "The only lesson I learned is that you can't be trusted and I'm sick of fucking listening to your poisoned words." I called out to my magic, asking it to wake up. My hands burst into purple flames.

Her eyes widened but she seemed amused by my actions, not scared. I didn't give it a second thought, a foolish mistake. I cupped my hand, making a ball of raging fire. I pulled my arm back to throw it at her, to end this war, end the suffering and pain. The fireball left my grip but instead of shooting towards her, it was blasted away by an invisible force. I watched it explode against the far wall, right before I was flung into the hard surface of the wall.

I should've seen it coming, I was sloppy in my anger. I smashed into the wall forcefully. The air was knocked out of my lungs as my head spun from the crash. I was on all fours as I looked to the source of the attack. A small woman stood near the dais with her hands outstretched.

"A wind elemental. So handy to have. Fire, earth, and water are also a great resource for a queen to possess." Tatiana spoke the words confidently as another woman entered the room along with two men.

Fuck.

Before I could gather my wits, I was hit in the ribs by a powerful jet of icy water. I felt a few ribs break under the immense pressure. I yelped from the sudden pain and blinked back tears as I glanced at Tatiana.

Her lips parted in a cruel smile. "I had hoped to invite you to join the others. But I have a feeling they would end up dead in their beds with their throats cut, as would I. I can't have a pet that would turn on me if given the chance, which sadly means you are no longer useful to me, at least not alive. Bring me her head."

Fear. For the first time in my life I was feeling true fear. I was scared. My heart raced as panic set into my bones. In that moment, I remembered Caleb. How frightened he was all the time, but he never let it show or cloud his actions. He always appeared strong and brave, even when he wasn't. I couldn't let Tatiana get the best of me.

The next moment a fireball exploded next to my face, bits of stone debris and embers flew into my eyes, blinding me for a few precious seconds. I scratched at my eyes as they burned, trying to regain my vision. The ground rumbled and I was bashed against the walls repeatedly.

I desperately flailed around trying to right myself. I'd been in hundreds of fights but never against four elementals set on killing me. If I couldn't steady myself, if I couldn't get my shit together, I was going to die here next to the other woman.

My hands went up to block the next ball of flames from striking me. It exploded close by, but I wasn't burnt yet. I threw out a wave of power to buy me some time. I needed to escape, I could handle maybe three to four guards or one elemental but not more than that. I'd never trained for this. The elementals were supposed to be dead, not helping Tatiana.

The wave knocked the four elementals back, as well as the handful of guards still in the room. I didn't look toward the throne, I couldn't be concerned with Tatiana right now. I looked to the doorway I'd entered through, but the hall was filled with armed guards. I'd never make it. The other way out was the side door, but I didn't know what I would find on the other side of it. I'd have to take my chances and hope for the best at this point.

I got up on wobbly legs and sprinted to the door. My right hand was a few feet from the knob when a large rock came out of nowhere and hit my open hand with a force I'd never experienced before. My hand shattered instantly, the skin the only thing holding the pieces of bone together. I screamed out, clutching the now useless hand tightly to my chest.

Trapped. I was trapped like a wild animal waiting for the hunter to make their final move. I needed to focus and not give in to the panic filling every fiber of my being. Words that were easier said than done when everything in my mind was fighting to stay alert and sane.

I was blasted with more frigid water. It pushed my body against the side door. The water pelted my face, making it impossible to breathe. Only water rushed into my nose and mouth. My lungs begged for air, but water was the only thing that filled them. Where the fuck did this asshole get so much water? My mind began to fade, the edges of consciousness dulled. No...no. I had to stay awake, even if I felt the other side calling out to me.

The cold wet stream stopped, and I fell limply in a heap on the floor. I couldn't move, water leaked out of my mouth. I pulled my eyes open, just barely slits. There, on the ground, was bloody water pooled by my face. So much water...so much icy salty water. The ocean.

I didn't question it. Fight, flight, or freeze. My basic instincts kicked in and said it was time to take flight. I must have moved just enough that they knew I wasn't dead yet. Hot blistering flames tore into my right side. My skin cracked and bubbled, I could faintly smell the charring of flesh, *my* flesh. I wanted to give in to the warmth, let everything go. The pain was a tether to this life, this existence. Was I ready for the tether to break?

I propped myself up on my elbows and weakly pulled my knees under me. I crawled slightly, coughing up blood and water onto the already soaked floor. I heard a distant clapping, was that applause? "My, my. I am pleasantly surprised. I didn't think you'd last this long, I'm almost a tad sad to see you go. Oh well."

I didn't look at her or them. I kept my eyes firmly on my exit, I gripped the wall and pulled myself up slowly and painfully. I rested my back on it, finally peering at my attackers through swollen eyelids. I reached deep inside of myself to that last piece that clung to life and lashed out with it. They were flung backwards, and Tatiana was ejected from the black throne. I inched over a few feet to my left. From this view I could see Tatiana lying face first in the pool of blood from earlier.

She whipped her head around to me, her face coated in the woman's blood. This time Tatiana didn't contain the fury she tried to hide, now it was displayed for all to see. I smiled at her, a mischievous little grin. My eyes moved back to the elementals. The first woman that had attacked me had recovered herself. I planned on her gathering herself first, she was my way out. Her arms went up and her palms faced me. She let out a surge of air, and I braced myself for the impact.

It blasted into me, but I had placed my body in front of one of the floor to ceiling windows. I went out the two-story high window, flying backwards through the air as glass shards accompanied me. *Thud.* Fuck. It was worse than when I landed in the Old Forest, at least the moss floor had cushioned the fall that time. I sucked in a breath of fresh ocean air as I blinked tears from my eyes. A searing pain in my back to the side of my stomach told me I landed on some glass.

Movement from the upper window let me know it was time to go. Flipping onto my side and I managed to get myself into a standing position. My fingers numbly pulled the glass shard from my lower back, and I pressed down with my left hand to staunch the flow of the now bleeding wound. One foot fell in front of the other as I hobbled away. Decent progress was being made when a sudden sound sent pure dread down my spine.

A drakyn roar. Tatiana's drakyn had been gone from its nest near the gates. In my haze, thoughts of its presence had been forgotten until this moment. I ran. I was already wounded, and in absolutely no shape to take on an angry drakyn. I pushed my legs to go faster. My freedom lied just up ahead. It wasn't much farther; I could make it. I *had* to make it.

Wings beating in the distance grew closer, as its roars shook the ground beneath me. I could hear the buzz of its mind, it was focused on one thing: *kill.* No, thank you. I hadn't made it this far just to be eaten by a blood thirsty beast.

I was twenty feet away. The bellows of anger grew as did the speed of the flapping wings. I could feel the air from them on my neck. Ten feet. The word became clearer. *Kill,* but it was Tatiana's voice. Five feet. Its breath was warming up my backside, I could hear its teeth biting for me. One foot. I was there, freedom. It was inches from me, while the drakyn was a mere breath away.

Right as its jaws were about to close around me, I jumped. I leapt off the cliff that overlooked the Auria Ocean. The drakyn's talons scraped along my shoulder, cutting into the flesh. The creature was upset at the sudden disappearance of its prey. It circled back for me, but I was already plunging into the icy water. My body went into shock, my mind went fuzzy then black. But I clung desperately to the tether holding me here.

Chapter Six

I was bashed against the rocks unapologetically as I floated wildly in the water. The ability to think or function was lost as I drifted on my back. Bright skies turned dark blue filled with shining stars. My eyes closed and I drifted in and out of consciousness. How long had it been since the cliff? I couldn't be sure as another sunny day beat against my eyelids. My body floated limply, I didn't fight the current or try to swim, what would be the point of expending what little energy I had left?

I slipped back into the void, finding comfort and refuge there. Time lost its meaning, the only notice I took of its passing was my growing hunger pangs. I pushed that away; pushed aside the agony from the gash in my side, the burning in my skin, the deep cuts on my shoulder, and my numerous broken bones rubbing together in ways they weren't meant to. I continued to flee into the abyss, the place where my mind existed but my body didn't. I could escape the pain for a while and keep my sanity somewhat intact.

It was in that place that I was disturbed by a strange sound. I didn't want to leave the peaceful void, I didn't want to feel my body and how broken it truly was. But the noise wouldn't go away, so I came back to my mind and physical body. I groaned softly as everything screamed out in agony. I focused on the sound. Was that…voices?

"Ahoy! Are you alive down there?"

I ever so slightly turned my head and peeled open my crusty eyelids. I was met with the sight of a ship, an odd one. Mostly men and a few women had their heads peering over the side at me. I wanted to answer but my throat was raw from the attack at the palace and going days without any water that was safe to drink.

A small rowboat suddenly appeared next to me, or maybe I had drifted off again, I wasn't sure. A handsome man looked down at me from his seat. He studied me head to toe, then looked at the others in the boat.

"Hello there. You are alive," he said in a friendly manner.

"…un-unfortunately," I gritted out.

He chuckled. "By the looks of you I'm sure death would feel better at the moment. I must ask though for my sake and my crew's, who do you serve?"

I was confused by the question, and I could feel the darkness creeping back into my mind. I stuttered out one word before I lost consciousness completely. "…m-myself."

I felt the rolling of waves beneath me but then the creak of a ship accompanied them. I was dry and warm for the first time in what felt like a long while. My eyes opened to take in my new surroundings. A decently comfortable smaller sized bed held me currently. A deep midnight blue blanket covered me—it was incredibly soft, I'd never felt such a nice material before. To my left was a porthole window. It was dusk, day giving way to night as dusty rose merged into regal purple.

An old oil lamp on a nearby post swung rhythmically back and forth. I was mesmerized by the moving flame, so much so that I hadn't looked around the entirety of the cabin.

"You're awake."

The words made me jump, sending pain shooting across my whole body. I turned my head to the right, where a wooden table full of food and drink stood. The source of the voice was shrouded in shadows, the oil lamps near them were not currently lit. I tried to speak but my voice was no more than a hoarse croak.

The mysterious person grabbed a metal dented pitcher of dull silver and poured some clear liquid into a similar looking cup. They walked around the table over to my bedside. As they came closer, their face was illuminated by the light from the flickering flames. It was the handsome man from the rowboat. He appeared to be in his mid-thirties with dark brown-ish black hair that fell in wisps onto his forehead. He had the start of a beard and beautiful deep ocean blue eyes.

He had a friendly smile upon his lips as he held the cup up to my parched mouth. "It's water, you need to drink it."

The cold liquid felt glorious as it soothed my raw and aching throat. I greedily drank the whole cup down. He gave a laugh when he realized I swallowed all the water in a few gulps.

"Figures you'd be thirsty."

I licked the last few droplets from my lips, making sure I got every single drop. "How'd you get the water to be cold?"

He gave a sly smile. "Just a little bit of magic."

My heart dropped. An elemental. Did he save me just so he could bring back as a trophy to Tatiana for her to torture? My eyes widened and I realized there were only a handful of exits, four porthole windows and a single door. I reached for my magic, but it was deep down within me, buried away. The fight against the four elementals and the time at sea had exhausted me more than I realized. I gripped the metal cup tightly, preparing myself for a fight with this man and more time in the frigid ocean. One good bash on the head should give me enough of a head start to escape.

He gave me a strange look before removing the cup from my clenched hand. "No need for any stupid choices like that. I'm not going to hurt you."

"You'll forgive me if I don't believe that for a moment," I stated as calmly as possible while my heart beat rapidly in my chest.

He smirked. "Not the trusting type?"

"It's my greatest flaw," I replied dryly.

He chuckled. "Is that your only flaw?"

"Wouldn't you like to know," I said curtly.

He sighed with a hint of seriousness. "I guess one can't be too careful these days. Especially someone special like you."

I swallowed down the lump in my throat. "Like me? I'm not sure what you mean."

"Right…" He leaned over my prone body and grabbed my left arm firmly. I tried to pull away but any effort to move reminded me that I was in horrible physical condition. He gently held my hand up as he pulled my sleeve down to reveal the intricate purple mark on my wrist. "I'll admit I've seen a thing or two in my long life, but it's been many decades since I've seen a mark like that."

I blinked at him, bewildered. "You've met someone else with this mark?"

He ran the pad of his thumb along the delicate lines. "Yes. She was a kindhearted woman, though fiery when provoked. I-it doesn't matter now. I'm aware of what the mark means."

I glanced at his fingers still touching my mark. "How much is Tatiana offering you for my return?"

He scoffed. "She doesn't have enough gold to afford someone like you. Even if she did, I'd be a shitty person to give you to her. She'd either torture and kill you or eventually figure out what a powerful elemental you could potentially be."

I rolled my eyes. "Yeah, super powerful, that's why I can barely move a muscle in my body. I've been fighting most of my life, almost daily. I was an unbeatable champion...now I'm a nothing. They wiped the fucking floor with me." I stared at the wall, not wanting to look at the face of the man.

He was quiet for a long moment. Then he said in a near whisper, "Even the strong have to experience moments of weakness. How else would they learn to grow? You should try to rest and heal." He stood up and turned the knob on the oil lamp, plunging the cabin into shadow.

My mind wanted to protest but my body was thrilled with the idea of sleep. I didn't respond to the man, so he took his leave of the room. The door clicked shut behind him as I laid there in limbo, that strange place between wakefulness and sweet slumber.

My thoughts ran untethered, replaying my pathetic attempt at saving the woman who had stolen food for her children. I wondered if they were okay or waiting worriedly for their mother to return. I should've left, I had let my anger and cockiness get the best of me, let it cloud my better judgement. I thought it would be simple to walk into the palace and rid Tileon of Tatiana. I was stupid to think it would be that easy or simple.

The memories of the fight rippled over and over again as I remembered the pain. But mostly I was ashamed of how weak I felt in those long minutes. I thought my magic would protect me like it had when I dealt with Pyron in the past, but it hadn't. I felt utterly alone, unworthy of the title of artifact of the Vayu.

My body felt heavy yet weightless as I drifted off into a restless sleep. Unfortunately, my dreams were plagued with visions of blood and the sharp talons of drakyns ripping into my flesh.

A salty breeze wafted into the cabin through the window near the bed. I opened my eyes to take in the warm sunshine that filled the room. Birds called out to one another outside as they flew freely throughout the morning skies. I laid there, staring up at the ceiling, breathing in the scents that reminded me of home. They were mixed pleasantly with the aroma of wood and other smells I couldn't quite identify.

I was putting off the inevitable. Eventually I needed to get out of this bed. My bladder was screaming that it was full and my stomach growled with hunger pains. I had been putting it off, I knew the elementals had caused some significant damage to me, but I was terrified to assess how bad it truly was.

I sucked in a deep breath, mentally preparing myself for the certain pain. I flexed my feet and ankles carefully, a twinge of unpleasantness accompanied it—just sore muscles. Next I wiggled the fingers on my left hand gingerly, they were okay. My right hand, however, wouldn't move, the hand was still broken into pieces. I used my only good hand to feel around my body. My right side was in a bad state. Major burns extended from my thigh to my shoulder, they were slimy with a sickly-sweet scent. They were definitely infected. I wasn't shocked, ocean water was not something you'd want to soak in for days on end.

An odd protrusion in my upper stomach area drew my concern—broken ribs. It hadn't pierced through the skin but that didn't mean it wasn't causing some unknown issues to my insides. My hand moved to my lower side on the left, the gash was still there from the glass shard. It wasn't as long as I thought it had been, but it had pierced through my back to stick out the front of my stomach. Slowly I raised my hand to touch my left shoulder. Pain shot down my arm and side as I grazed my fingertips across the gouges of flesh. My jaw clenched, remembering how close I came to being a drakyn's meal.

I'd been mere inches from certain death. Maybe I still was, my wounds were massively infected, and I wasn't healing like I normally did. Since the match with Mr. Fire Elemental, I'd been able to heal quickly. Minor cuts and bruises were gone within a day, more serious injuries had taken a couple of days at most. I'd never had an infection before, only seen the other fighters get them.

I didn't make a sound as tears streamed down my

temples into my dirty hair. I began to worry that it had all been a strange joke or a huge mistake, perhaps both. I wasn't truly the artifact or anything remotely spectacular. When I had needed them most, my abilities weren't there to save me from the elementals or Tatiana's drakyn. They didn't help me while I floated lifeless in the vast ocean or heal me when I was the most broken I'd ever been. Who was I or what was I without my gifts? How was I supposed to save Tileon when I could hardly save myself?

The door creaked wide open, interrupting my deary thoughts. I turned my head ever so slightly to the right to see who my visitor was. The man who had rescued me appeared along with an older woman and a young boy, who were both carrying trays. The familiar man came to stand near the foot of the bed.

"Good morning. You look…rested today," he said with a forced smile.

I narrowed my eyes at him. "Excuse me for looking a touch rough around the edges."

He raised his eyebrow and gave me a once over. "Just a touch?"

I gave him a dirty look. "Didn't realize I was supposed to be getting only beauty sleep."

"You don't need any beauty sleep from where I'm standing," he said with a playful wink.

I felt my cheeks flush, but the woman's stern voice cut off my reply.

"Is now really the time for flirting?" she asked him with a disappointed look.

"Just trying to keep her spirits up."

"Sure you were." She brought over her tray. It was filled with medical supplies of all kinds. She placed it at the foot of the bed, then motioned for the young boy.

His tray held a bowl of water, a cloth, and a small glass vial containing a milky green liquid. The boy set the tray at the woman's feet before scurrying from the cabin.

"This is Ira, she is a healer from Keme. She can hopefully help ease some of the discomfort you're in." Ira was an older woman, perhaps in her seventies, with long curly white hair and dark weathered skin. Her eyes were a light green with a playfulness about them. She wore jewelry that contained various stones, though I was unsure of what type they were.

I looked at him. "I get to know her name before yours?"

Ira looked between me and the man, before rummaging through the items stacked on her tray.

He chuckled. "Apologies. In all the excitement of your presence I have forgotten my manners. I am Captain James, and you are aboard the Mischief." He gave a showy bow. "And you are?"

I bit my lip, not sure if I should lie or be honest about my identity. I'd never been afraid to tell anyone my name, but now I wondered if it would be foolish to offer up such valuable information. My gut told me I could trust the captain and Ira. "Niya."

The older woman instantly stopped fiddling with the various items on the tray and stared at me wide eyed.

James's smile vanished. "Your name is Niya?"

I knitted my brows together. "Yes?"

He glanced at Ira, then back to me. "As in the former queen of Azzaria and rumored princess of Mageia?"

I looked at both of them surprised. "...yes. How do you know that?"

"We know many things. We've certainly heard of you.

At least the interesting gossip that has spread throughout Tileon," James stated.

"Oh. Trust me, I'm hardly worth such gossip," I said, uncomfortable that they knew things about me that were untrue or highly exaggerated.

"Somehow I doubt that. You seem very fascinating to me," James said with a smirk.

Ira gave him a pointed look. "Enough questions for now. Let's see what we can do about some of this mess. It'll be a painful process, but this should take some of the edge off. Drink all of this." She handed me the vial of gross looking green liquid. I put the small glass vial to my lips and swallowed the contents in one greedy gulp.

The liquid burned going down my throat. The sensation was unpleasant at first but soon the warmth spread slowly throughout my body. My head turned fuzzy, the edges blurred, and it took my pain to a dark distant corner of my mind. Everything was clouded in a haze, and I was grateful for it as Ira began to poke and prod at my wounds.

Ira and James spoke but the words slurred and made no sense to my drug addled mind. Not that it truly mattered at this moment, I was too busy enjoying the relief from my injuries. I was more than happy when a dreamless sleep claimed me.

One minute I was dead to the world for all intents and purposes, and the next I was wide awake trying to orient myself back into my body. It was a huge adjustment, going from feeling absolutely nothing to feeling everything all at once. The suddenness was jarring to my senses but as I slowly settled back into my skin, I only felt some residual lingering pain. It was nothing like it was before. The stench of rotten flesh was gone, replaced with a fresh clean linen smell and the scent of clean bandages.

I flexed my broken hand, and this time I felt the small quiver of movement. It wasn't much but it was better than a limb that wasn't able to hold a sword any longer. The burnt slimy skin was removed, replaced with the start of new flesh. It was sore and raw to the touch as new nerves tried to repair themselves. It was an unpleasant feeling, but I was incredibly thankful to be rid of the infection. The gash in my side and the multiple wounds on my shoulder had been expertly stitched up.

I took a deep breath, then lifted myself into a sitting position. It took a long few minutes of struggling and a few angry tears to accomplish. It was exhausting and I wanted nothing more than to lay back down to sleep forever. I pushed away the tired feeling and swung my legs over the edge of the bed to plant my feet firmly on the ground.

I gave a tentative feel of the soundness of my legs and feet. My toes wiggled on the worn rug that covered the cabin's floorboards. I added a bit of pressure before attempting to stand up. I wobbled and fell back, then gritted my teeth together and pushed myself back up. I braced my good hand on the bed frame, steadying myself and letting my feet get used to holding me up again.

With baby steps, I made it to the edge of the bed. It was a small goal to achieve, but I was very proud of making it. I was grinning like a fool when the door opened, and James came in.

He raised his eyebrows at me then smiled broadly. "Look at you, standing up like a big girl."

I rolled my eyes. "Can't kill Tatiana by laying around in your bed all day, can I?"

He pursed his lips as if deep in thought at the question. "I suppose not. But I can think of other things you could do while laying in my bed." He waggled his eyebrows suggestively.

I laughed at his implication. "While I'm sure you could find dozens of women that would gladly take up such an offer, I'm not one of them. I have to help Tileon."

His smile remained but it turned sad and his expression became serious. "I must say that's a first."

"A woman turning you down?"

He gave a humorless chuckle. "Well yes, but that's not what I was referring to. I've never seen someone near death fight to get better just so they can return to the dangerous situation they almost died in. Most people in your position would protect themselves."

I sighed heavily. "I'll admit that thought has crossed my mind more than a few times. I'm beyond terrified to encounter those elementals again or a drakyn. But I couldn't live with myself if I chose to do nothing. Yes, I could protect myself, but who protects those that can't protect themselves?"

"You could die this time."

I nodded solemnly. "I know, but at least I'll have died trying to save our world."

He looked at the floor. "All hail the rightful queen."

"I'm just me. I don't care about any titles." I thought about Marcus and the others living under the Swords and Sin. He hated his life currently but had grown content to hide away.

"Which is why you deserve them."

I smiled at him as my legs buckled beneath me. My

hands flew out to catch myself. Before I could hit the floor, strong arms caught me. I winced in pain and sucked in a sharp breath. I looked up and was face to face with the captain. His ocean blue eyes roiled like stormy water.

His face was mere inches from mine. "Time to put you back to bed."

"I guess..." His scent wafted up to me. It was a wonderful mix of salty sea breeze and old aged wood.

"I admire your desire to be completely back to your old self. But you are going to need some time and lots of patience to fully heal. Ira will attend to your wounds a couple times a day to help speed up the process."

His hair brushed against my cheek. My face heated uncontrollably. "What happens then?"

"You tell me." He glanced at my lips then back up to my eyes.

"Then you need to return me to Azzaria."

He looked puzzled. "Why Azzaria?"

"That's where my destiny is."

CHAPTER SEVEN

The days turned into weeks aboard the Mischief. Ira came every morning and night to check on my healing progress. She was pleased with how far I had come in just three weeks. I was less than happy with how I had healed. I wanted to be the way I was before, physically and mentally.

"I think our time is coming to an end," Ira said joyfully, pulling me from my musings.

I looked at her alarmed. "I'm still hurt."

She frowned. "My queen, I've done all I can for your wounds. They are as healed as they will ever be without some special magic I do not possess."

I played with the corner of the blanket I was snugly wrapped in. "I understand…thank you Ira for everything you've done for me, it's beyond appreciated."

She nodded and left me alone in the room. I closed my eyes as a few tears escaped down my cheeks. I opened and closed my right hand shakily, it hadn't mended correctly at all. It was no fault of Ira's, the hand had been shattered, the small pieces of bone weren't able to heal to the way they once were. I was lucky to have the limited use of it I did possess, but I could no longer hold a sword with it.

I got out of the bed I'd grown fond of. Though I felt slightly guilty that I'd taken over the captain's quarters for so long. James had never commented on the subject, nor had he made me feel unwelcome on his ship. In fact, he seemed to enjoy having me aboard and if I was being completely honest with myself, I liked being here too. It felt like an escape, a place far removed from the horrors of Tileon.

I exited the cabin and walked down the small hallway to the step ladder that led up to the main deck. The deck was bustling with life as men and women prepared the ship to get as close to Azzaria as they could. Then James would attempt to get me to the entrance of the sewer tunnel. I hoped Marcus and the others were still living in the underground chamber. I didn't want to consider or think about any alternatives.

I did my best to stay out of the crew's way. I stood by the railing just watching them. It was fascinating to see them working in perfect harmony together. I turned around, staring out at the open water that laid before my eyes. It was so calm and serene today. Not a single cloud was in the sky, the sun shone brightly, warming my skin and making the ocean sparkle brilliantly.

"Beautiful, isn't it?"

I didn't need to glance over to know who the voice belonged to. "It is absolutely gorgeous. Peaceful."

He leaned his elbows onto the railing. He was wearing a black shirt that left his arms and shoulders exposed. His markings were on full display, sweat glistening on them as he stared at me. "You'd be surprised how peaceful it can be out here. How safe it is."

I spoke softly. "I know."

He let out a frustrated sigh. "It's not my place to tell you what to do. I understand why you want to return home, truly I do."

"But?"

He smiled. "But I wish you would stay. There are more lands than just Tileon. You don't have to fight a lost war or die for nothing. We could travel somewhere new, somewhere safe."

I stared out across the calming water; I couldn't look at him or I'd be more than tempted to say yes. "I can't. Not because I don't want to. But it would haunt me to abandon Tileon like that. I wouldn't be happy with myself, and the guilt would consume me no matter where we went or how far away from Tileon we traveled."

"I was afraid you'd say that." He said it in a disappointed but understanding way. "The offer will always be there for you. I hope you'll one day take me up on it."

"If the last few years have taught me anything, it's that you never know what the future could hold."

The corner of his mouth tugged up in a lop-sided grin. "Is that a maybe?"

I returned the small smile. "It's definitely a maybe."

He nodded absentmindedly. "We should be close to Azzaria in about two days, then me and you will take a rowboat the rest of the way. I have to ask, what happens if Marcus isn't there?"

I shrugged. "I'm trying not to think about that possibility. If they aren't there, then I'll figure out a different plan I suppose."

"I'll help you as much as I can, you know that, right?"

I looked at him. "You've already done so much for me

already. Now you're putting yourself at risk by taking me home. I won't ask anything further from you."

"We are making this choice because we believe in you even if you don't right now. As far as we are concerned, you are our queen, and we support you."

I gave him a worried glance. "I don't want anyone getting hurt because of me."

He gently brushed a stray hair out of my face. "This is war Niya. Removing Tatiana is going to be a bloody affair, people are going to get hurt. They've been suffering for no reason for years. You'll give them a cause that's worth fighting and dying for."

I placed my hand on top of his. "I wanted to avoid that part of war. Wanted to take care of it on my own."

"I know but fate has a different path for Tileon's future."

"Hopefully fate knows what it's doing. I sure as shit don't."

He chuckled loudly. "Not knowing is half the fun, the journey is the other half. Things don't always go as we wish them to, but that's what makes life worth living."

"I'll have to trust you on such things old man." I laughed at his sour expression.

"Ouch, you wound me with your lack of manners. Get some sleep, it might be the last decent rest you'll get for a while." He squeezed my shoulder and went back to work with his crew.

I smiled as he walked away then looked back at the endless ocean that was ripe with limitless possibilities yet to be discovered.

• • •

The sky was a deep midnight blue dotted with countless sparkling stars. They were amazing to look at, and I wondered what mysteries they held beneath their glimmering light. We had waited until night was at its darkest to launch the small rowboat. We didn't take much with us, just what I had brought on to the ship when I washed up near it and enough supplies for James to make the trip back.

He had given me explicit instructions before departing. The biggest rule was to stay completely quiet, any sounds would travel loudly across the water for quite a distance. So, we rowed along in silence with the only noise coming from the oars going in and out of the still water. The rhythmic rowing was calming, the consistency of it lulled me into an almost sleepy state.

My back was towards Azzaria. I instead watched the Mischief fade into the nighttime darkness. I felt a pang of sadness at leaving it behind. Once it was out of sight, I kept my eyes focused on James. I was filled with doubt at the road ahead of me. At what my destiny would hold for me, for Tileon. I was filled with uncertainty, but I had promised myself I'd take it a day at a time and leave all my worries to deal with at a better time. Right now certainly wasn't the time to be filled with worry and be unfocused.

As the shore grew closer my heartbeat picked up, and I bit my lip. James noticed and gave me a worried look. A weak smile was my only response. The waves crashed on the beach and the boat started rocking harder. James jumped into the water, pulling the boat onto the rocky shore.

I hopped out so he could secure everything. I looked around, making sure there were no patrols that we hadn't spotted when rowing in. When he finished his task, he came to stand by me.

He whispered softly, "You sure about this? We can still turn around and be back on the Mischief in no time at all."

"But then you did all that rowing for nothing." I smirked.

"Well, you can watch me row some more if you'd like." He raised his eyebrow in a suggestive hint.

I shook my head with a giggle. "Perhaps another time. The tunnel entrance is this way. You sure you want to come with me?"

"Very sure. If anything happens, I'll be here for you."

I started walking toward the hidden access door before suddenly stopping. James bumped into me. I threw him an incredulous look over my shoulder. "Why did you row us?"

He looked completely confused. "It's a rowboat, usually you row them."

"You're a water elemental, you don't need to row anything. You could've pushed us along with your power, which would've been quieter than the oars."

The confused look morphed into a sly one. "Then you wouldn't get to see me put my muscles to work."

I scoffed and smacked him on the arm. "Unbelievable." I shook my head and walked toward the tunnel.

He chuckled under his breath, and I could hear his footsteps following mine as we got closer to the hidden entrance. There were stacks of boulders and vines completely covering the large rocks. I went around a few of the stacks to part the overgrown plants. I walked through them and held them open for James.

We were plunged into a dim darkness as the vines fell

closed. "Ugh, what is that vile reek?" James gagged slightly as we entered the sewer.

I laughed. "You don't want to know. This was the sewage tunnel for the establishment above."

I couldn't see his face, only heard the crunching of his boots on the random debris. "How do you know about any of this?"

"I used to live here. Before the war, before I was named queen. I was just me, nothing more, not a princess or a savior. It was nice."

"What kind of establishment was this exactly?"

I smiled more to myself than to him. "It was a whore house, among other things. You probably would've enjoyed it."

His footsteps immediately stopped. "You were paid for...sex?"

I gave a hearty laugh at the awkward way he asked. "No. I worked in the fighting pits and, at times, the blacksmith shop."

"You were a slave then...I'm sorry. I don't mean to sound so surprised. I had heard rumors about the new queen of Azzaria but didn't pay them any sort of credit."

"It's okay James. It made me stronger in a lot of ways, made me who I am. Though I do wish I had been trained like you, to be able to control my abilities."

James resumed his walking. "I could find you a teacher, or try to. Your gift is unique but there's someone out there that must know how to help you hone it."

"That's nice of you to offer. You are a charmer, aren't you?"

"Only when you're around."

I rolled my eyes in the near dark. "The gate should be just up ahead." We walked about fifty feet before we came to the metal gate made of bars that Tyrone had put in place to keep people out from the lower levels should they ever stumble upon the tunnel. No one ever had but it also made for an excellent escape route if one was ever necessary.

The gate was still chained shut but the bottom corner was bent up enough that a single person could wiggle their way through.

"Please tell me we don't have to actually get down into the fucking filth and crawl through that shit?" James asked, disgusted.

I tossed him a pitiful glance. "Then I won't tell you… just show you." I got down on my knees and close to the hole in the bent gate. I turned onto my back and wiggled through the gap slowly. Once I was on the other side, I waited for James.

He was less than thrilled to scoot his way through the gate. It took him a lot longer than it had me due to his larger size. He was a head and a half taller than I was and all his years of labor had made him a well-built man. It was entertaining to watch him struggle through the muck.

"I've got to say, that was fucking awful. I need a hot bath," he said as he tried and failed to wipe himself off.

"You needed a bath before," I said jokingly.

He gave me a dark look. "Aren't you funny. How much farther?"

"We are about halfway there. There's a few bends then a straight shot to the main chamber."

"Are there anymore nasty gates to crawl underneath I should know about?" James asked, annoyed.

"No, just that one. Don't be such a grump, it's only a little shit soup."

"Easy for you to say, you got less on you."

I started to walk ahead. "You'll be fine."

"Maybe if you gave me a rinse off." He chuckled.

"Sure, I'll give you a rinse with a bucket full of sludge."

"Down girl." He paused for a moment, all amusement gone. "I don't hear anything. That's not a good sign," he stated low enough for my ears to catch.

"Maybe they're being cautious." We trekked on as quietly as possible. When I knew we were near the main chamber, I pulled out my sword with my good hand. James also pulled out his, preparing for the worst.

As we came into view of the large room, we noticed a dim glow coming from up ahead. I looked at James, he held a finger to his lips then hugged the walls as we both crept up to the tunnel opening. We stood at the edge where the wall of the tunnel met the large chamber. I took a risk and peeked around the corner.

I pulled my head back and put my sword away. James looked uncertain and kept a firm grip on his weapon. I stepped out from the shadows into the dimly lit room. My sudden presence was met with a shriek and a dish being dropped onto the floor, breaking into dozens of pieces.

I put my hands up in a peaceful manner. "I'm not here to hurt anyone. It's me, Niya."

The older woman in front of me was shaking uncontrollably, and I felt bad for scaring her. Lady Trina looked around nervously, then answered me. "I-I-I'll get Marcus. He was just leaving for a hunting trip."

I nodded and put what I hoped was a friendly smile on my face. "Thank you."

She quickly departed through the rusty door that separated the sewers from the basement area. I tossed a look over my shoulder to the shadow filled tunnel. I knew James was standing there, waiting to make sure I was safe. Neither of us had said anything about it but I wasn't able to handle myself like I once did. I couldn't fight six guards alone anymore.

The door creaked open, and Marcus rushed through it. Before I could utter a word, he had his arms around me in a tight embrace. He pet my hair in a soft caress as Theo walked into the chamber. He looked at me like I was a ghost that had been haunting him for years materialized in front of him at last.

Marcus's words were difficult to understand as he spoke them into my hair. "You're alive. I-We thought the worst." He pulled away to look me over and smiled.

Theo found his voice. "My lady…how?"

I moved away from Marcus's embrace and glanced behind me. "I had some help."

James stepped out of the dark tunnel and into the light. He looked at me with his eyebrow raised and gave me a cheeky grin. "It's always a pleasure to help the royals of Azzaria."

I shook my head at him. "James found me floating pretty much dead in the ocean. He was kind enough to nurse me back to health. He also took a huge risk to bring me back here."

The joy on Marcus's face twisted into a sneer. "How kind of him. Hopefully there weren't too many pleasurable moments."

James looked like a cat with a mouse. "Can you really have too many when the delightful queen is around?"

Marcus swallowed down a reply as Theo elbowed him in the ribs. The old advisor seemed genuinely happy to see the ship's Captain.

"James, I didn't think we would run into you again. Especially under these circumstances," Theo stated gleefully.

"It's good to see you again old friend. I'm sorry to hear the years have not been kind to you and your charges," James said to Theo in a friendly way.

"We are thankful for your generosity. We don't have much, but we have a few coins to spare."

James cocked his head to the side. "That's not at all necessary. My help was offered freely to Niya. I don't want any payment for doing what was right."

"You're a good man Captain. Can we offer you some food?" Theo asked.

James perked up instantly. "I'd love a warm bite to eat." He looked at me. "You should eat something as well."

I nodded absentmindedly. "I will, don't worry. I have a couple of questions first."

Marcus focused his attention back on me. "Ask anything. Not sure we can answer them, but we will do our best."

"What happened after that day in the market?" I had wanted to know for weeks.

Marcus took a deep breath. "We watched from the alley when you killed those soldiers. We saw the woman take off down a side street and then you went up to the palace. We waited for you to return but instead we saw guards come from the gates to hunt down the poor woman. Then almost an hour later Tatiana's drakyn flew over the market in a frenzy. We hid until it was dark out, then returned here hoping you'd be here somehow. But that never happened. Days turned to weeks without any sign of you. Tatiana put that woman's head on display but didn't make any announcement about you or your fate."

I looked down to the ground. "I tried to save her. To save Tileon." I rubbed my right hand, remembering the pain of it breaking into tiny pieces. "I thought I could kill Tatiana by myself, and everything would be okay."

Marcus stared curiously at my hands but didn't ask about them. "I know you meant well. I wish you would've taken her life that day and rid us of her presence. But I'm very grateful that she didn't kill you, that you're here."

"She almost did. I barely made it out. I don't know how I survived," I said quietly.

Theo shifted uncomfortably from foot to foot. "I don't want to come off in any way insensitive but…how did you lose? You are supposed to be the most powerful elemental alive…"

I looked at James, a water elemental who truly was powerful. He gave me a weak smile. I shrugged and sighed heavily. "I don't know why you would think that."

Theo and Marcus shared a look. Theo answered. "We were told that you were."

I knitted my eyebrows together. "By Tyrone? He just likes to brag about my skills, since he likes to take credit for them."

The two men shook their heads in unison. "He does talk about your legendary weapon skills frequently. But the person who said you would save us and Tileon with your abilities was Kaia."

I looked at the men, suddenly very interested in Kaia again. "Where is Kaia?"

They looked behind them to a smaller tunnel that had a young woman's head poking out of it.

I pointed at her. "I need to have a word with you."

CHAPTER EIGHT

Kaia's eyes widened in surprise. "Me?"

"Yes, you. We need to talk, just the two of us," I responded, giving a look to the three men. Marcus and Theo seemed unsure about me speaking to her alone, James was merely staring at Kaia, like he was trying to figure her out.

She gave me a weak nod. "Okay."

I left the men to talk amongst themselves, or make snide comments, and walked over to where Kaia stood. "Is there somewhere we can talk privately?"

She glanced around the somewhat crowded chamber. "Not down here, no."

I knew a place we could talk alone, but I wasn't happy about it at all. "Follow me." I didn't check to see if she was behind me, I just assumed she was. I went to the rusty door and carefully opened it without a squeak. I walked into the basement area, then dragged my feet as I traversed the stairs. Flight after flight we went up until we reached the very top floor. I stopped for a moment, remembering how this hall had always been filled with laughter and music. The only sound now was the soft whistle of wind going through the drafty windows.

I started moving again, taking care to keep my eyes on the well-worn red carpet that lined the hallway and not on the dozens of empty rooms that were on both sides of the corridor. I'd known most of the girls who had occupied these spaces, I didn't know how to comprehend that they were gone now.

I reached the end of the long corridor and pushed open one of the already cracked doors on the right. It held two beds that were unmade. Clothes littered the floor and the scent of old musty incense hung in the air. I went to the bed closest to the far wall and hovered at the foot of it. My fingers touched the dirty blanket thrown carelessly in the middle of it.

"You've been here before?" Kaia asked in a hushed voice.

I turned to look at her. "This was my bed. It doesn't seem like much, does it? But it was my home."

She studied the small room and went over to the bed opposite mine. She gestured to it. "May I?"

I shrugged. "Up to you. I don't think its former owner would mind."

Kaia sat down carefully on the edge of the mattress, her hands delicately folded in her lap. "It's funny to me, how different yet similar we are. Both princesses in our own right and born to someday rule, with gifts considered extremely rare. But our lives turned out so differently."

I stayed standing with my hands on the foot board of the bed. "You were raised as a royal with a castle and family. While I lived here. I'd say your life turned out better."

She held a faint smile on her pale lips. "You have

humble beginnings. You needed them to grow strong. Besides in the end we both ended up in the same place together, did we not?"

I scoffed. "Right."

"You disagree."

I didn't answer her, I wasn't sure what I believed anymore. I once was very certain of my opinions, now, I didn't know if I truly knew anything anymore.

"May I speak honestly?" she asked.

"Of course."

Her smile grew. "I figured you'd appreciate such things. With all respect due your titles, let it fucking go already."

I was actually speechless. I blinked stupidly for a solid minute trying to process if I heard her correctly. My eyebrows were near my hairline when I finally stuttered out a reply. "E-Excuse me?"

"You heard me," she said simply.

I narrowed my eyes in disbelief. "Well then. Straight to the point."

"You can take it how you wish. I'm here to help but no one can do anything for you while you cling desperately to everything you're holding on to."

Perhaps I didn't want to speak honestly with her. "You don't fucking know me."

She laughed bitterly. "That's where you're wrong. I've spent my life having dreams about you. Seeing all the things you've done as if they were my own memories. I've grown up watching you, I know things the others don't. Things not even you allow yourself to acknowledge completely."

I swallowed hard, feeling an uneasy mix of fear of what she knew and discomfort that she was aware of things not even I realized. I felt exposed to her, and I didn't like it one bit. I made my way to the side of my old bed and sat down heavily, a puff of dust springing into the air. We sat facing each other.

She continued. "I know about Caleb and the sacrifice you had to make regarding him."

"It had to be done," I said with as little emotion as I could muster.

She looked upset. "It did unfortunately. Your souls are bound together tightly but your fate lies in this time frame, this lifetime. Leaving him behind…that took a strength very few possess. You did what was right even if it was a steep price, a piece of your soul."

"The choice had already been made for me in a way. I had read the history books in Heka. He was meant to marry Brisa and have a son with her. I don't pretend for a second to know how my power works, but I don't think it can change history."

"You'd be right. People think they have free will, the ability to make their own decisions, but they don't. The important pieces have already been written by fate, only the minor parts can move around slightly."

I looked down at my hands; one rough with calluses, the other a tangled mess of skin and bone. "You think I can save Tileon?"

She seemed to choose her words carefully. "I think you have the will and ability to do so, but not in the state you are currently in."

I let out a laugh devoid of amusement. "I'm doing my fucking best."

She tilted her head just a touch. "You were already broken before the incident with Tatiana. A painted plate with minor cracks running throughout it. Pieces chipped off in large chunks after the events involving Alec and Caleb. Tatiana only shattered you further. You just need some strong glue to put you back together and to remember who you are at your core." She got up from the bed and knelt down in front of me. "You are still that woman that fought in the pits, who kicked everyone's ass for years. You were undefeated for a reason, that woman wouldn't sit around afraid of a rematch. She would train day and night until she knew she'd win." I was startled when she took my hands in hers. "Alec would not want you to punish yourself every day for his death, you weren't to blame. As for Caleb, he knew in his heart you had another war to fight. That wasn't goodbye for you two, you'll have another cycle together."

A tear escaped and ran down my cheek. "What if I'm not powerful enough to beat Tatiana?"

Kaia brushed the tear away. "It's not about power, you have that. It's strength of will."

"What if I can't get mine back?" There it was, the question I couldn't ask out loud to the others. But with Kaia I let my walls down, she already knew the worst about me, what was a little more?

She glanced up at me with a expression of absolute pity. "Then we stay under Tatiana's rule and Pyron stays in charge once more."

I gazed up to the ceiling. "No pressure."

"I believe you'll find your way again. You're just taking a little detour."

My eyes met hers as my heart thumped in my chest quickly, I wasn't sure if I wanted to know but my mouth asked anyway. "Have you seen how it ends?"

Her lips turned into a grim line. "Yes."

I squeezed her hands in reassurance. "Can you tell me what to do? Where do I go next?"

Her face lit up a smidge. "During the final battle, I see you surrounded with purple flames and a massive white drakyn flying above you."

I smiled, of course. "Thank you, Kaia. I know just where to go." I gave the younger woman a tight hug. "I appreciate you believing in me, even if I'm not there yet."

She hugged me back. "We all get lost, but our path is never too far from us."

I stood up and gave the room a once over. It had been my home, my safe place, but it didn't feel like it belonged to me anymore. I wasn't the same woman anymore. Kaia was right, I was holding on to my old life. A life that no longer existed.

"What now?" Kaia asked curiously.

"Now I start packing for a long trip. I have a drakyn to see."

Kaia and I talked a few hours longer. Discussing both my life and hers. I asked her about living in the sewer chamber. She said it was difficult, especially with Marcus and Annabelle constantly fighting, but she kept going in the hope that it wasn't forever. I recalled Annabelle's remarks when I had first returned, I was curious at what had happened between the couple, but I wasn't going to ask Kaia for the dirty details.

Talking to her had helped me more than I wanted to admit. I'd let Tatiana beat me mentally, made me question who I was in the worst way. I had bogged myself down with so much guilt over things I had little to no control over.

I realized that the moment Marcus had stepped foot into the Swords and Sin, the war had officially begun. I had made my own choices to the best of my knowledge at the time. Just like Alec had, he wanted to be a part of my journey and wouldn't be persuaded otherwise. Instead of being thankful for the time we had together, I'd been dwelling on his death and not the life he lived. Who was to say he wouldn't have died here in Azzaria fighting against Pyron?

Caleb had also made his own decisions. He knew I was in the past to find the artifact and stop the war in my time. When he found out I was the artifact, I think deep down he knew I'd have to leave but not in the cowardly way I'd chosen. That part did make me feel bad but what was done was done. I couldn't change it at this point.

I was Niya. The undefeated champion of the Swords and Sin, a princess of the lost land of Mageia, rightful queen of Azzaria, and the artifact of the Vayu.

Who was Tatiana compared to me? A tyrant ruling through bloodshed and fear that was keeping my throne warm. She was hurting my people, they deserved better, and it was time to pull my head out of my ass and fight for them.

Kaia and I went downstairs to the underground system. When we entered the room there were more people occupying the space. I was wrapped up into an enormous hug that was accompanied by the sounds of sobs.

Tyrone clutched me to him as he cried uncontrollably. "I thought I'd lost you again when Marcus told me about you going into the palace. How could you be so stupid?"

I gave him a dark look. "You taught me to always go for the throat, no matter the cost. That's what I did, it wasn't my fault that she surprised my ass with four elementals. I was under the impression that they were all dead, not working for her."

Tyrone gave me a guilt-ridden look. "I didn't mean to sound rude, you're all I have left."

I stepped away from him. Time may have softened him and his memories, but he had been a harsh master, even if he treated me kinder than he had the other girls. I hadn't forgotten the treatment I had received from him. "You don't own me any more Tyrone. We weren't friends, I was your slave. You only liked me because I made you filthy rich. If I hadn't, I would've met the back of your hand and belt more often than I did."

Tyrone glanced around at the others. "That was a long time ago, I was a different man then."

"Perhaps it's been a long time for you, but it hasn't been for me. I'm not beneath you anymore, do not speak to me like I am."

For a second, he appeared to be angry then his face took on a defeated appearance. "Understood." He left the group and went into one of the side tunnels.

"Well that was terribly awkward." I turned to look at the owner of the voice. The king of Aquaen was an opinionated man, who made his thoughts well known. I personally found him refreshing.

"It wasn't for me," I stated blandly.

Landen burst into laughter. "I must say I'm so glad you are alive and kicking. Five years with only these duds for company has grown dreary."

The others tossed him a glare, however I smiled—I saw where Kaia got her personality. "Sorry to disappoint you but I'm not staying."

Marcus looked shocked but Landen merely grinned at

Kaia. Marcus voiced his obvious displeasure at my sudden announcement. "You just got here, you can't leave."

"I can and must. I came here to find my path going forward and I've done that. This war isn't over and I'm not done fighting. But there's somewhere I need to go before I can help Tileon fully."

James spoke up. "Then let's go, I'll take you where you need to go."

Marcus's face turned stony. "I know the land better than you do, I can take her where she needs to go."

James pursed his lips in a mocking way. "I can get her places you've never even dreamed of."

Theo rolled his eyes and spoke softly. "Must we have a pissing contest?"

I shook my head and my eyes met James's. "Actually, I need to speak with you alone." I gestured to the foul tunnel that we had entered through.

He grimaced. "There's really no other way out of this place?"

"Afraid not captain. It's just a bit of muck and grime," I teased the water elemental. I gave him a couple of minutes to say his farewells to his old acquaintances.

We went back through the tunnel again slowly. I once more watched the large man struggle to get past the small gap in the gate. He wasn't amused with me giggling at his discomfort.

Once I could see the slight hint of dawn beginning to break, I stopped. James looked at me, understanding spreading across his features.

"You're not coming with me."

I was grateful for the semi-darkness. I felt a tug of sadness at seeing him go. Being around the captain and on his ship was familiar, it was comfortable. Sending him away was anything but easy for me. "No, I'm not."

He was upset at the news. "I was hoping you'd take me up on my offer."

I tried to put on a brave face. "I know you were, but I'm needed here. I do need a favor from you however."

He gave me a half smile. "Name it."

"You've traveled around Tileon…and other places. The place I'm going to is far from here, but when I return, it'll be to finish this war. I want you to find others that would be willing to join us. Maybe other ships."

"I can do that. It'll take time though."

"That's okay, I'm not sure how long I'll be gone, could be a few weeks to a month or two." The way time worked in the Hall of Doors was still a mystery to me.

His smile widened. "I'm a patient man with a lot of time on his hands."

I matched his smile. "We will see each other again James."

"Promise?"

"I can't promise that but as long as I'm alive and you are, I know we will eventually meet again."

"I very much look forward to that day," he said wistfully.

I don't know why I felt compelled to do it, but I stepped close to him. I placed my hands on his chest and got on the tips of my toes to place a kiss on his cheek. "Thank you."

All the bravado was absent when I stepped back. "What was that for?"

"I don't know, just because I suppose." I shrugged.

"Well I'll take it. Please be safe Niya," he said quietly.

I nodded. "I will for Tileon's sake."

He barely shook his head. "I don't care about Tileon, I care about you. I doubt I can save you twice."

"I'll be as safe as I can. Don't worry, I'll see you soon James."

He pulled me into a hug, it lasted for a while. Then without another word he placed a kiss on my forehead and departed through the vines. They swung closed behind him.

He was off to find others for my war against Tatiana.

I gave myself a moment to steady my emotions. I pulled myself together and went back to the chamber. When I got there, Marcus and Theo both held packs in their hands.

"What's going on?" I asked loudly.

Marcus held out a second pack to me. "We are going with you."

I shook my head vigorously. "Absolutely not. It's too dangerous."

"We understand the danger my lady," Theo said.

"I—"

Marcus cut me off. "We are going with you. This is our war to fight, and we've been sitting on the sideline for a long time. Let us help you."

I caught movement out of the corner of my eye. It was Kaia with her eyebrow raised.

I sighed, knowing an argument would be pointless. They would just follow behind me either way. "Fine, we leave tonight, be ready."

Chapter Nine

Night fell in Azzaria, giving us the perfect cover of darkness needed to make our way out of the city and into the forest. We pulled our cloaks tightly around us as we crept through the forest that bordered Azzaria. I was anxious we would run into soldiers patrolling the area, but Theo assured me that they didn't travel out here anymore. There was no need to, everyone who had rebelled was dead as far as Tatiana knew.

Who did Pyron have left to truly fear at this point? Even so, we remained vigilant while traversing the forest. It took us days of slow-paced travel to make it safely to the edge of the Old Forest. Theo and Marcus became nervous the closer we got. They feared Mageia, especially the magical forest that drove away unwanted guests. Alec told me how hard being within Mageia's borders had been. For him though it was the Ayu that kept him up at night. He would catch them out of the corner of his eye but never figured out what they were.

I gave the two men a pitying glance as I stepped into

the Old Forest. The pine and evergreen trees had given way to twisted trees of unusual colors. Plants unique to this land grew in abundance along the ground despite the lack of sun that filtered down. To most it was dark and frightening here, to me it was a safe haven.

We walked along the path that wound its way through the trees. I was ahead of Marcus and Theo by quite a distance. I stopped to let them catch up to me and when they did, I noticed they both wore strange expressions.

"Is everything alright?" I asked, confused by their faces.

Theo's eyebrows knitted together and he looked around wildly, at what I wasn't entirely sure.

Marcus seemed to be on the verge of a panic attack. "I don't feel anything."

"Lucky you," I replied sarcastically. I wasn't someone who enjoyed being emotional, or having to console someone who was.

Marcus huffed at my words. "I don't feel…crazy."

I glanced between him and Theo. "Okay…you're acting a little crazy. Should I leave you two alone to talk?"

"What? No," they both said in unison.

"Well you guys are acting strange."

Marcus rolled his eyes. "I meant I don't feel anything like I did every other time I've been here."

I finally understood, they weren't feeling anything while in the Old Forest. "That's not a good thing."

"Speak for yourself," Marcus snapped.

"I am." I gave him a dirty look. I remembered him being a lot nicer years ago. "That feeling you felt when entering was protection magic. The fact that you feel nothing at all now…"

"There's nothing left to protect?" Theo asked.

I shook my head. "There're definitely still things here to protect. It means there's no magic left. Mageia's magic is tied to Tileon, the war and death of so many…I think the magic is gone or close to it."

"How bad is it going to be with no magic left?" Theo asked.

"I honestly don't know. I'm not sure if we can even get to the place we need to go without any magic." I was nervous the door that led to the Hall of Doors wouldn't open anymore. Would any of the arches?

"Should we turn back?" Theo asked quietly, but I heard him nonetheless.

I stared off in the direction of the ruins, a place that seemed deserted, broken, and worthless. A facade to protect the truth; to hide elementals, Vayu, and free roaming drakyns. I was placing my blind trust into Kaia's hands at the moment. "You can return if you wish to do so but I'm going to keep going."

Marcus quickly spoke up. "I'm not turning around. If you're still continuing on, so am I."

My eyes slid to Theo. He was watching Marcus closely. "Let's keep going shall we, we are losing the light."

I gave them both one last look before returning to walking on the path. Theo appeared to be keeping a close eye on Marcus. I didn't blame him, he was different and Kaia had said he was struggling with the situation they were in. Raising a family in that place would make any sane person bitter. Annabelle was obviously angry with Marcus, for what reason I wasn't sure. The last few years had been insanely rough for everyone.

I chose to keep my distance; I didn't need any drama or petty fights to contend with. I wanted to stay focused on alternative plans should the doors and arches not work any longer. So far, I'd come up with absolutely fucking nothing.

I was happy to have some company, even if it was Marcus and Theo. I didn't want to do this alone, not yet. It would take more than just me to help Tileon recover. Even if we won this war, we had a lot to do to rebuild all the lands.

It had been a quick couple of weeks. We weren't slowed down by the Ayu at night or the magic that caused the two men to struggle before. Instead we rushed along, only sleeping for a few hours at a time before continuing on. I wasn't sure if it was wise to push ourselves so hard, but I couldn't truly sit still. In those moments of rest, my mind raced vividly with too many thoughts to fathom. I desired nothing more than the opportunity to shut off my mind, if only for an hour or two.

I focused on our surroundings, recognizing this place. I'd been here more times than I wanted to be. My mouth felt dry as I stared stupidly at the entrance to a supposedly small cave. I internally cursed this place, its very presence a reminder of past events I'd love to forget. The two men didn't seem to notice my discomfort. They were busy with their excitement at the discovery of the dry lodging.

Marcus sighed with relief as he took it in. "Wow, look at this place. This will be perfect for shelter."

Theo nodded with relief. "Indeed it will be."

They were beyond thrilled while I stood completely unimpressed by the cave. I remembered the first time I had seen this place with Alec and felt the same thoughts. The feeling of finding a dry place to sleep that wasn't out in the open. Those days within the cave and with Alec were wonderful moments that I cherished fondly.

However, the same couldn't be said for the time I spent here with Caleb. That time was less than pleasant, torture that went on for hours or days. I don't remember how long it went on for. And quite frankly, I never thought to ask. It was a thing that caused Caleb pain to talk about and caused me pain to remember. To be completely honest it wasn't something I really wanted to discuss. I swallowed down the dread as I looked around the grass, the trees, and the plants surrounding this place. How innocent it all looked, but I knew better. I knew what had happened here so many years ago.

How Pyron had brutally butchered countless lives in the vain hope that they could squash the remaining rebellion. They had hoped and failed. Was that a good sign for our cause? Or did it mean that eventually more would die here? Would more innocent blood be spilled in this spot? I hoped not.

I swallowed down all the emotions I was feeling and finally spoke up. "This spot would be great. We can stay here a day or two. Perhaps have a fire. There should be water around here somewhere. Maybe find some food. I haven't seen much out here alive except us."

Theo nodded. "Yeah, I noticed that. Not many birds or other animals wandering around in the Old Forest. Is that due to the lack of magic here?"

"I'm not sure, but if I had to venture a guess, I'd say it's a strong possibility," I answered.

"Well, hopefully it's a good sign and not a bad one," Theo replied.

Marcus found his voice. "Why don't me and Niya go

make a fire. Explore the cave a little while you gather some firewood?"

Theo nodded and headed off into the twisted trees to find some dry wood for us to burn. Marcus and I went into the darkness of the cave. The front area was lit slightly, while the back was dark and mysterious as always. I looked around on the floor, where there were remnants of fires long ago put out.

"This seems like a nice place," Marcus stated as he looked around.

I muttered, "Seems like it."

Marcus scrunched up his face. "Have you been here before?"

I looked around and started grabbing random pieces of splintered wood. I quietly put the kindling together to build a fire. I didn't look at him as I answered. "Once or twice."

He squatted down next to me. "Not good memories, I take it."

I looked at him out of the corner of my eye. "No, not good memories. I don't really want to talk about it."

He took the hint. "Fair enough. So how did you learn to build a fire?"

"From a really close friend of mine. Took a long time to learn unfortunately. Hopefully I still know how to do it."

I flattened out a patch of dirt and made a mound with the pieces of wood and twigs I had found. All I needed now was for Theo to come back with some firewood and we would be set for a day or so. There was enough kindling to start a fire, just not enough to keep it going all night. I scraped wood against wood and gave it a small burst of magic. Fire sprang to life. I stared into the flames and became lost in the memories of the past. I closed my eyes trying to push them away.

I suddenly felt a hand on my shoulder. "I'm sorry for what you went through."

My breath came out slightly shaky and I took a seat on the dirt ground. "We've both been through things. I haven't had to endure the last five years like you guys did."

He fully sat down as well. "I know but I can't imagine what you had to experience."

"It was nothing," I replied.

"It was something. I heard what you said to Tyrone. Your friend died from an arrow." He looked at me curiously. "He was just a friend?"

He didn't fully understand the implications of the question he just asked. My eyes never left the flames as they flickered. "He was more than a friend to me. But I lost him just the same."

"I'm sorry for your loss."

"It was what it was," I said with as little emotion as I could muster. "If there's anything I've learned, it's that no matter how much you try to save your loved ones, in the end, it feels like in order to win this war, you have to make sacrifices. And not just people..." I lowered my voice. "...but yourself as well."

I could feel his eyes on me. "What do you mean by that?"

"You don't feel it? How different we all are. Not one of us is the same person as we once were."

He thought about it briefly. "I'll agree with that. It's hard to hold on to yourself when all your hopes and dreams are ripped away from you."

I pursed my lips. "Is that what it is for you?"

He huffed. "Yes. I always thought that I would be this great king if Pyron ever attacked us. I would easily defeat them, would push them back to their borders. Overall be this great man. Instead, I watched as one by one all the lands fell away. Aquaen is a broken shell of what it once was, and I wasn't there for them. My own land I stupidly lost."

I gave him a curious look. "I've been meaning to ask how that happened. I've got to say I was beyond shocked you didn't fight."

He gritted his teeth together. "It wasn't my choice."

"No?" I raised my eyebrows.

He shook his head. "It was Annabelle's."

"Oh…" I was finally starting to understand why he was angry with her.

"Our people always voted on things of importance that involved all of Azzaria. If it affects all, it should be decided by all. There was a vote held on whether we should fight or run. Instead, during the meeting, surrender was proposed. I never even thought I'd hear such words during a time of war." I didn't say anything as he clutched his arms around his knees. "Before I knew it, we were voting. I thought the whole time it would be unanimously in favor of fighting. Fighting for our people, our lands, not giving up to Pyron. Allowing Tatiana to take over and kill like she did. We only got a few votes for our cause. When it was asked who was in favor of surrender imagine my surprise when I turned my head and Annabelle had her hand up. I know she wasn't alone in her vote. I know that, but she had always been the first to say we should fight. The first to say we would be okay and there she was deciding she wanted to give up." Marcus let out a bitter laugh. "I knew in that moment."

"Knew what?" I asked.

"I knew I had made a mistake."

I was extremely confused. "How so?"

"She wasn't a queen. Not really. She should've known better. Instead, she thought we'd surrender and go on with our lives as if nothing ever happened. She really believed that we would be allowed to live in the royal chambers. Be Tatiana's prisoners for the rest of our lives. How stupid does that sound?"

I could hear the rage in his voice. I now knew why they had been bitter towards each other. Annabelle had decided to surrender Azzaria to Tatiana, while Marcus wanted to fight. He blamed her for what was going on.

He continued his story. "Once Tatiana did lock us up, Landen and Kaia helped us escape. If it wasn't for them, we'd probably be dead. Theo would be for sure, he had been locked up in the dungeon along with the rest of the council. We never saw it, but she put their heads on spikes. The first ones she put there. The years have been long, I tried to move past it, I did. But I kept returning to the fact that I wanted the opportunity to try. Maybe things would've ended up the same. We could have fought and lost anyway. But we live like rats in a sewer, my children have never seen sunlight. All because their mother couldn't discuss something with me. Why was she afraid to tell me that she felt worried."

"I don't know." It was all I could say, I didn't understand why she wouldn't talk to him about something so important.

"I wish you would've been there."

"I doubt I would've been much help," I said simply.

He looked at me. "Would you have surrendered?"

I couldn't look at him. "Does it really matter at this point?"

He looked back at the fire. "No, but I already know the answer would be no. You wouldn't have run away either."

"I ran away when she attacked me."

He shifted uncomfortably. "I know, but you went in and attacked her. You were willing to go in there and do what it took to end this war. You didn't expect her to have elementals at her side. Had she not? You would have won this war for us. You would have won for Tileon. You didn't hide behind some stupid notion that everything would be okay. You're a fighter."

No response came from my lips nor did I feel like saying anything further. I didn't want to say anything negative about Annabelle, especially when I didn't really know her except for secondhand knowledge of her. Even if she was angry with me when she had seen me, I can't say that I blamed her. She didn't expect the life she had and to spend so many years pretending to be me. To have her husband look at her with anger in his eyes. And I could only imagine that it had been said once or twice out loud —that if I had been there in her place, things would have been different.

How long had she been comparing herself to me? Her a maid who grew up in the palace cleaning up after the people that were now her family, and me, a woman who grew up in a fighting pit.

It was in my blood, my drive to fight. I had forgotten that until Kaia reminded me. Even then, I couldn't imagine sitting around doing nothing or willingly surrendering myself to a life living the way they were. No, that wasn't me. Perhaps it was the Vayu within me or the artifact, or it was just who I was. I could never give up to someone like Tatiana.

We sat in silence and then something I wasn't quite expecting, something that caught me off guard for a moment, happened. I felt his lips press into mine. His warm breath was ragged as his heart raced. After a moment of shock, I kissed him back. It was different, friendly, then he deepened the kiss.

Eagerness and haste overcame him. His hands cupped my face as his tongue explored my mouth and soon his hands trailed down slowly, stroking my back. He started touching me everywhere, discovering my body as he kissed me like it was the last thing he was going to do in this life.

His hands roughly gripped my shoulders, and he pushed me toward the ground. Soon his body was pressing into mine, and I felt the hardness in his pants rub against me in rhythmic strokes.

It was nice, nice to be wanted. It was simple, no complications. I let my hands freely roam along his body, it wasn't well muscled, his years of starvation had taken a massive toll. His mouth finally left mine and I sucked in a breath of air. He began trailing kisses across my face and down to my neck.

He came to where my top concealed the rest of my skin and slowly pulled it back, exposing the flesh there to him. In that moment, everything screamed inside me. Flashes of Alec's face sprung into my head only to become muddled and transformed. Forest green eyes bore into mine as I remembered Caleb. The love I had for both of them washed over me.

This wasn't right, I didn't love Marcus, I hadn't ever

desired him in this way. I had only thought of him as a friend. I pulled away as much as I was able to.

"This isn't right."

He mumbled into my skin and continued placing kisses along my neck.

I shook my head, trying to clear it. "No this isn't right."

He lifted his head. Gray blue eyes met mine and I knew right then that we had to stop.

His eyes were filled with a haze of desire. "It's okay. You have no idea how long I've wanted this. How many times I've thought about us together."

I shook my head harder. "No. Annabelle."

"Annabelle and I aren't like that anymore."

I pushed him off of me and he flew back into the dirt roughly.

He stared at me wide eyed. "What's your problem?"

"My problem is that you have a wife, Marcus, and children," I said slightly out of breath.

He glared at me. "You are my wife. Annabelle and I never had real vows."

"That's a nasty technicality," I said incredulously. "And while we did take vows, we've never ever been more than friends. You two have been so much more than that."

"Then why did you kiss me back?"

I looked at the ground. "I don't know, but I shouldn't have."

"We can though, it's okay."

I shook my head firmly. "We can't ever be like that. I am trying to fight for Tileon, for our people. I don't have time for other activities. My focus has to be on the war and winning."

He stared at me darkly, anger burning in his features. The heat of his desire still bulged against his pants. His mouth parted to say something when Theo walked through the cave entrance with firewood clutched in his hands.

He looked down at Marcus then over to me. "I found some dry wood." He held up the wood he gathered awkwardly.

I nodded briskly and stood up, walking over to help him. "Thank you, Theo. This looks great." The words were just a little too high pitched and cheery.

He glanced down at Marcus who stood up quickly and walked hurriedly out of the cave. I bit my lip without saying anything.

Theo just made a disappointed face at Marcus's retreating back. "Are you okay?"

I shook my head and then nodded. "I'll be okay. Just another bump in the road, nothing to worry about it."

He put on a fake smile. I could tell he wasn't completely convinced, but I wasn't willing to discuss it with him.

We spent the rest of the night in quiet solitude. Marcus sat outside the cave, while Theo and I sat inside near the fire. I didn't know what to say to either one of them, so I said nothing. Shame burned through me at the mistake I almost made.

After spending a night in the cave awkwardly with Marcus pouting outside the whole time, we continued our journey. The men talked to each other, but for the most part I was left alone with my thoughts, and I was perfectly fine with that. I was filled with thoughts of my previous journeys; when me and Alec first discovered the ruins, then when I helped Caleb save the remaining rebels.

As we grew closer to what many knew as the heart of Mageia, the two men perked up in excitement. I hadn't had the heart to tell them that the ruins were a facade. Perhaps hundreds and hundreds of years ago it had been an actual city and home to the once powerful kingdom. But now, it was nothing more than something to deter people from coming here. From asking too many questions and finding the true heart of Mageia.

I also didn't tell them that this is the place where Alec's last moments were, I didn't want to get into it. I truly didn't want to think about it ever again. I did glance briefly at the disturbed mound of dirt where I had buried him, it looked like any other bare dirt patch. If you didn't know what you're looking for, you'd miss it completely. An entire life reduced down to nothing more than an unmarked grave in some random ruins that weren't even real. The thought made me sad, but I pushed the guilt away.

We were so close now. So close to where we needed to be. Theo and Marcus looked around, their eyes wandering over every single building. They seemed to want to explore desperately as they touched and searched through the ruins.

I rolled my eyes at them. "There isn't anything here really to explore. It's just a bunch of buildings." I didn't stand around to watch them, instead I headed straight for the one building that I knew we needed to go to. A place that truly had all the magic hidden deep within. I walked to the nondescript door and opened it. A plain door for a plain building. I doubted anyone would guess that it held a massive secret inside.

The two men followed me reluctantly, seemingly unhappy to leave behind the ruins so quickly. When they entered the boring building, they looked around, confused.

I chuckled, more to myself than to them. "This is the way, you'll see."

I placed my hand upon the back wall that looked like nothing out of the ordinary. A deep rumble started from within the ground and the stone wall opened to reveal the ancient staircase that led mysteriously into the darkness. Both men backed up instantly.

Theo spoke with a frightened tone. "We have to go down there?"

I smiled and nodded. "Yep." I grabbed some torches from my bag that I had made while we were stuck inside the cave, in preparation of the dark staircase, and handed them to Theo and Marcus. I lit them with a little burst of magic, and while still holding a small ball of purple flames in my hand, I stepped inside. "Are you staying here?" I asked.

They glanced at each other and then took a deep breath. Theo was first to go in, slowly walking step by step down into the darkness, his torch clutched firmly in his hand.

Marcus hovered on the landing for a moment, then stared at me. "You know I'd follow you anywhere. I trust you with my life."

I only gave him a blank look. "I know." I gestured towards the slippery steps, part of me hoping he'd slip and it would knock some sense into his head. "Go."

He made his way behind Theo, and I stepped out of the way of the door. It closed with a final thud that echoed through the hallway. We made our way down the stairs and into the Hall of Doors. Marcus and Theo looked at each door, studying them and peeking inside a couple of rooms where the doors laid wide open. Curiosity got the better of them at what magic could do. With how many secrets this world truly held.

Before we knew it, we were standing in front of the bricked-up doorway that would take us to the place I needed to go.

Marcus's head swiveled over to look at me. "You're joking. How are we going to get through there?"

"With a little bit of determination." I put my hands on both sides of the bricks as the men moved to stand down the hallway, looking concerned. I pushed on the wall, which did nothing. I pushed again, this time putting a bit of my magic behind it. It gave a little but not enough to break through. I stood there for a minute, then closed my eyes, remembering all of the hurt that was bottled up inside of me. Then I pushed out a large blast of magic.

The bricks gave way, exploding into the room beyond. The room's air felt incredibly dense, with a thick sluggish quality to it. I hated being in this room, it filled me with nothing but dread. As I walked into the pitch-black room, I was reminded of how it held an inky darkness unlike anything I'd ever seen before.

The two men carefully followed behind me, their torches blowing around wildly as they entered the room. Fear lit their features as the firelight danced upon their faces.

Marcus whispered, "I hate to ask this but where the fuck is this place?"

I whispered back, not wanting to disturb the air, "I don't have a name for it. It appears to be just a room." I placed my hand where I knew the archway was. There was a bit of simmering magic and the little, tiny bowl popped out from the wall. "Well, here goes nothing." I hoped the magic was strong enough to transport all of us to the jungle land.

I pulled a small dagger from my thigh pouch and slid it across the meaty part of my palm. The blood of the Vayu dripped into the bowl. A little rumble accompanied it as the bowl gave way to a simmering blackness of pure magic. The doorway that held the jungle world indeed appeared. I gave a nod towards the archway and they both looked at me wide eyed with their mouths hanging open.

"You're kidding," Marcus said loudly.

"No, I'm not. This is the only way."

Theo steeled himself for the trip, but before he could walk through, he grabbed Marcus by the shoulders and pushed him in. We watched as the shimmering black magic swallowed Marcus.

Theo stood there as the arch's magic played across his features. "Any advice for the other side?"

I shrugged. Nothing could really prepare you for the feeling of going through the arches, especially someone without any magic in their body. "Just be grateful you didn't have a big lunch." I pushed the old man into the dark swirling magic and took one more glance around the dark inky-ness of the room before stepping through myself.

Chapter Ten

We came out on the other side roughly. I wasn't fond of the feeling of nausea that accompanied going through the arches. I'd wanted to give Theo and Marcus a heads-up on what it would feel like when they arrived on the other side but decided against it. It's one thing to be told about it and another to experience it. What very little lunch they had in their stomachs ended up sprayed across the grass.

They both glared back at the arch with narrow eyes. Marcus choked out a few words. "What was that?"

"What little magic exists in the world," I stated.

They both crouched in the thick grass gathering their bearings. As I looked across the jungle land, I sucked in a deep breath of hot humid air. I forgot how thick the air here could be, it wasn't light and breezy like in Tileon. Here you could feel it in your very lungs, a wet smothering sensation.

I listened to all the various noises that now filled my ears, the sounds were vastly different than the ones in Tileon. Even after visiting Heka, this was such an unusual place, it was unlike anything I'd ever seen, at least in this lifetime. A small part of me enjoyed being here, while another larger part felt uneasy. I'd gotten somewhat used to the scenery last time I was here, but these two stood completely awestruck as they took in the jungle land for the first time.

I felt a touch guilty for not explaining anything to them. What was here, what could be here, who could be here. I didn't have the capacity, the time, or the patience to explain the journey in detail. Maybe I wanted them to experience it like I had. Traveling to a strange new world and seeing it for the very first time was exhilarating.

I noticed it had changed since the last time I had been here. It was always difficult to determine how much time passed whenever I went through an archway but to me the jungle looked bigger and more grown out. The insect and animal sounds remained the same as the portal whooshed shut behind us. Only a stone arch stood in the middle of all the trees and lush grass.

I glanced back at the two men. "Feeling better?"

They both gave me a look. Marcus answered coldly, "Thanks for the heads up."

I shrugged. "I figured everyone should experience it that way at least once."

"What is this place?" Theo asked.

"I'm not exactly sure. I've only been here once before."

Theo raised his eyebrow, curiosity etched into his face. "Alone?"

I shifted from foot to foot. "No, I came here with a few others. There were rumors about this place, that there were evil magic users here. We never found anyone else or any signs of people actively alive."

Theo looked around warily. "I can't imagine that this place would be abandoned."

I agreed with him. "I'm not sure entirely. Just keep an eye out for any movement, in case they didn't brick up the doorway for no reason."

They both nodded and wiped vomit from their mouths.

Slowly we made our trek toward the pyramid-like structures in the distance. They both stopped dead in their tracks when they noticed them.

"What is that?" Marcus asked.

"There's quite a few of them. They're like pyramids. It's where we are headed," I responded.

He continued to stare at the multiple pyramids. "Is this Mageia?"

I shook my head. "No, this is somewhere else, trust me. Honestly, I think it's where the first people came from."

"Why do you say that?" Theo asked excitedly.

"Just some of the things I've seen here would make it seem like people were here, then left to Tileon. There's a lot of ancient items in one of the buildings; like gems, weapons, loads of old scrolls." I actually wanted to explore that structure and look at every space inside of it, but I didn't get the chance last time.

Marcus looked at me strangely. "Is that what we're here for?"

I wasn't ready to tell them about the white drakyn yet. "You could say that."

I walked away, ending any further questions they may have had. We trekked along in silence, keeping our ears strained for any sound from anyone else. All I heard was the jungle coming to life. Small bugs scurried from one place to another. Animals far away that were unseen to our eyes yowled wildly, making themselves known to us. I knew of the animals in the Old Forest, their noises a familiar sound to me, including the Ayu.

The Ayu was a beast dear to me, they wouldn't harm me, the opposite actually. With these mysterious jungle beasts, I wasn't familiar with how they behaved and was nervous to run into them. They were loud and at times I would hear the faint sound of their paws moving around, nails scraping against bark and brush being moved as something scurried past it. Every time I would turn around to spot them, they disappeared. I couldn't catch a glimpse of whatever was making the noises. Some moments it would be behind us, then to the sides of us. Other instances it would be right in front of us. Yet we still saw nothing.

The heat here was intense, especially when it mixed with the humid air. Sweat dripped down my back and my mind could hardly focus on anything else. The sun poured through the canopy in random spots, I walked carefully to avoid standing in it directly. I stayed where the leaves wound together tightly in an attempt to prevent the harsh light from reaching the dark wet dirt.

We were getting closer and closer to the pyramid-like structure that was nearest to us. The one that housed the white drakyn I needed to speak to. I was walking over a tree root when I heard it. One of the animal calls rang out but this time there was something else to it. Something that didn't feel quite right.

I stopped and glanced behind us. The two men nearly ran into me. They looked puzzled at my sudden halt and were about to open their mouths when I put a finger to my lips—shushing any words they may have spoken. My eyes scanned the distance. Watching, waiting, and observing everything closely. Did the shadows sit right or were they moving ever so slightly?

An uneasy feeling swept over me as if we were being watched and not just by animals. We continued our trek slower this time. As I watched one of the shadows intensely, I swiveled my head side to side, double checking that I hadn't missed anything. There, out of the corner of my eye, I saw the barest hint of movement. Too slow to be an actual animal, I knew for sure we were being watched by people.

My hand slipped to my side, grabbing the dagger there. I held it in my good hand. The magic burned through to my damaged one. My heart began to race as I prepared myself for what was about to happen. We were too far away now to run through the jungle and get back to the arch without an incident. I also wasn't going to leave here without the drakyn or at least talking to her.

Suddenly, without warning, a branch broke loudly to my right. Before I knew it my hand had flung the dagger. A piercing scream came from whatever I hit, and I ran towards it. Marcus and Theo were close on my heels. Ten feet away, covered in dark clothing that covered most of their body, was a person pinned to a tree, my dagger stuck deep into their arm. Their face was covered, only pale, orange-colored eyes were visible. They went wide as saucers in fear.

I began to ask them who the hell they were when I felt a warmth at my back. I turned my head to look behind me. People started emerging from the trees all around us. We were surrounded. Some of the people held flames in their hands, while some had little bursts of air swirling around them. Others had floating rocks, and a couple had water spinning in the air.

Elementals. I looked around at each and every one of them nervously. My purple flames sputtered in my hand erratically.

One of the strangers stepped forward and pulled down the covering that concealed the lower half of their face. It was an old man. He stared at me for a long moment, glancing between my face and my magic. He tore his gaze away from me to look at Marcus, then bowed slightly. "You're a long way from home."

Marcus squinted his eyes at the man, and in a shocked voiced replied, "Masou?"

I studied the strange man dressed all in black. He looked older than Theo by quite a few years. He had a weathered face that was etched with deep wrinkle lines. His skin was light brown with a golden undertone. His dark brown eyes watched us all carefully, mostly me.

My eyes flicked from Theo to Marcus. Theo's mouth fell open in bewilderment at the sudden appearance of this Masou.

Marcus's face held a stunned expression. "H-How is this possible?"

I glanced between them, not wanting to interrupt. I was curious how a man from the jungle land knew Marcus and Theo.

Masou answered, "I believe we have a lot to catch up on."

Theo nodded. "Indeed, it seems we do."

I looked around at the elementals still surrounding us with their powers on display. An odd sense of panic rose in my chest at watching them use their gifts. I did my best to swallow down the feelings that were rising within me. "Do they mind putting their fires and other stuff away?"

Masou smirked at me. "As you wish."

I did my best to keep my features neutral. "That would be nice."

All the different elements went out one by one and slowly the people disappeared into the trees as if they were never there in the first place.

Masou nodded his head toward the pyramid. "Follow me."

Slowly we made our way behind him as he walked through the forest. One step at a time, he led us closer to the structure. The whole walk there Marcus was in a state of shock, his brows deeply furrowed in silent thought. He would stare at Masou then around the jungle, as if trying to piece together their connection.

Marcus glanced at Theo and Theo just shook his head as if he didn't understand any of it either. We kept a healthy pace and soon arrived at the pyramid.

My eyes took in as much as they could of the giant structure. Even now I was still awestruck by the sheer size and beauty of it. "It looks spectacular," I whispered to myself.

Theo must've heard me because he turned around and smiled. "It is indeed. I've never seen such a sight."

We stopped at the base of the staircase that held hundreds of steps. I started heading for the steps that I knew led to the to the underground cavern of this temple, but I was quickly stopped.

"We are not going that way," Masou said firmly.

I didn't want to argue with him, but I also came here for this very purpose. "I don't remember asking."

He looked at me weary. "I understand you didn't, but

there is much we need to discuss before you make your journey into that temple."

I folded my arms across my chest. "Like what?"

"Well, for starters, we need to discuss what happened in Azzaria."

My heart sank and my breathing became ragged. "I'm not sure what you mean."

His eyes bore into mine. "I think you do." He turned and walked off.

I looked at the two men. We all stood there for a moment before they quickly rushed to follow him. I growled in frustration then sighed before following as well.

How did he know what had happened? As far as I knew it was a secret. I hadn't gone into detail or in depth with anyone. James knew the most, but only because he saw the condition I was in and made his own assumptions. I didn't want to discuss it, to share my failure. It was embarrassing to me. I was supposed to be powerful, yet I was beaten and broken.

We walked in a single file line behind the fire elemental until we reached our destination, which happened to be the other pyramid, or the temple that me, Caleb, and the other rebels had explored on our trip here.

I was fascinated by the fact that these were actively in use and not abandoned like we had thought they were. We walked up the many steps and into the building. The various rooms still contained all kinds of rare and unique items.

Marcus and Theo's eyes widened as they took in the gold and mass amounts of gems. The swords, bows, maces, and weapons of times long ago. Different pieces of art, sculptures, scrolls, books, and maps. Room after room, they were crammed full of different things. Who knew what you could find buried within the nooks and crannies.

I gave the room a once over before drawing my eyes back to Masou. He gave Theo and Marcus a friendly smile, but I noticed he watched me from the corner of his eye.

Throughout the room and down the hall were the other elementals. There were small groups gathered in key locations, such as certain doorways. They tried to put on an easy stance, but their posture was stiff as if they were standing guard waiting for us to leave. Or was it that they didn't want me to leave?

I gave an internal sigh of annoyance. The last thing I wanted to do was fight more elementals, but I wouldn't be stopped from getting to the white drakyn. I walked over to a table stacked high with piles of weapons and stood there casually. Just a simple stance of leaning carefully on the edge of the table. My hands crept slowly along the mounds of options. One pile of daggers caught my gaze and picked one up. Giving myself something to have at the ready if need be.

They instantly took notice of what I was doing, as hands went to weapons and different elements began to move around the room. Masou appeared alarmed, his face scrunched up. "We don't want any trouble or issues."

I put on an innocent smile. "Who said I thought you did?"

"Well, the way you're eyeing some of those daggers makes me wonder if you're going to do something we would both deeply regret."

My eyebrow raised. "I don't think I would regret it at all."

He looked nervous at the comment. "Perhaps not. But I

would like to speak with you first before we get to that point."

"Then start speaking. Like how you know these two?" I pointed to Theo and Marcus.

Marcus looked at me for the first time in a long time. He actually made eye contact with me, something he hadn't done since the cave disaster.

"We met Masou in Pyron years ago." I tossed a dark glare toward the fire elemental.

"It's not like that I assure you," Masou quickly added when he saw the look on my face.

"It was when I saw Tatiana for the first time in years. I had gotten injured by her drakyn and was sent to the sick ward in Fajro. That is where I met Masou. He was the healer there," Marcus clarified.

Masou nodded. "You are correct. At that time, I was the royal healer there."

My expression didn't change. "So, you're on Pyron's side."

He shook his head solemnly. "I'm on no one's side but my own."

"Well, that sounds familiar," I mumbled.

"I don't mean it in such a way, my lady."

I cut off his words. "You can call me Niya. I don't like formalities."

He bowed deeply, acknowledging my title with his gesture instead of his words. "Very well, Niya. When I went to Pyron it was not a choice I took lightly. But for all healers, no matter what, when they become Maesters they must journey to all the lands in Tileon to fully understand who they are, what they are, and how they function as a people. It's part of our training. So yes, I was in Pyron when I met the now King, to heal him."

My eyebrows knitted together. "How did you get here then?"

He grimaced. "An unpleasant story I must admit. We began to hear rumors about members of the royalty. Things from the sick ward started going missing from the cupboards. The kinds of things you'd notice if they were used. Different vials of poison were stolen in large quantities. Enough to kill a man or worse. We also noticed slight changes in the basic atmosphere of the city. People were becoming increasingly scared. Certain people that supported certain beliefs and feelings regarding the line of royalty started going missing. Before we knew it, one of our insiders came to us telling us that the King had been murdered. You can imagine we were not surprised she would do such a thing but still it wasn't something that we were prepared for her to do so soon. We escaped through a couple passageways that were known to us before we made our hasty exit."

I felt bad that he had known about Tatiana and her intentions but couldn't do anything about it. "So, you all ran?"

He looked ashamed. "Yes. We came here to stay safe."

Something bothered me about his story. "Wait a minute. You came here? How is that possible? Who are you?"

He knew what I was referring to, only Vayu could use the arches. "We are similar to you. Most are elementals but there are a lot of Vayu as well. Which is how we made it here to safety."

I looked around. "Where exactly is here?"

Masou gave a proud look. "This is Arcadia."

Marcus woke up at that statement. "This is the mysterious land of Arcadia?"

He nodded. "Yes, this is where we train and live without the concerns of Tileon spilling into our lives. Where we can keep to ourselves. Pyron can't storm in here and murder everyone without mercy. Only a Vayu can enter and typically they aren't on the side of a tyrannical ruler."

"Typically," I said.

He gave me a knowing look. "If I may be so bold, my lady Niya. I wish to speak to you, just us."

Marcus and Theo looked at me, perhaps expecting me to tell him no, perhaps expecting me to say that anything he could say to me could be said to them. But that was not the case. Some things I enjoyed keeping entirely to myself.

"Very well."

He spoke to my companions. "You two may stay here. Look through the items if you desire to do so, or we can have food and water brought to you."

Theo replied, "Food and water would be amazing."

Marcus gave me a look. It wasn't a very pleasant look, but I didn't dwell on it. I didn't give a shit that he was being kept out of the loop.

Masou led me to a different chamber room, this one far more ornate than the other one. This room was filled with different items. Items that felt strangely familiar, but they were not mine. I walked along the different shelves holding stacks of papers and ran my fingers across them. I closed my eyes as memories jumped out at me. Memories that were mine in a way but not from this lifetime.

"It must be an odd sensation," a voice stated from behind me.

I turned around, taking my hands away from the papers. The memories of the past faded away. "I'm sorry?"

Masou repeated himself. "I said it must be strange. To

have memories that belong to you yet are not your own, swimming around inside your head."

I didn't say anything, I wasn't sure what to say. "It was definitely not something I expected to ever deal with. That's for sure."

A ghost of a smile played on his lips. "No, no you did not."

"How do you know so much about me?" I asked.

"I know you've been to Heka a few times. I know you know certain things about yourself that could be dangerous in the wrong hands. Things you discovered while here in Arcadia."

"How?"

"We watched you closely when you came through the gate. We chose not to reveal ourselves to you at the time. You were not ready for such things, and your magic would've killed us most likely," he stated.

"You were there?!" I was angry that they had been here the whole time and didn't make themselves known to me. They could've been training me. My attention then went to the floor. I didn't want to know what he was going to say next, but I waited for it. "You know what I am."

His eyes studied me. "I know you're the artifact of the Vayu."

My heart thumped loudly. "Yeah, that was a lovely surprise."

He chuckled sadly. "I'm sure it was. I'll venture a guess that you expected it to be a charming, beautiful item." He picked up something random from the table nearby, something that easily could be used as a weapon. "A sword, perhaps something with more sparkle. The last thing you expected was for it to be you."

I shook my head. "No, I didn't. What's done is done, isn't it?"

"Yes, unfortunately. May I?" He reached out a hand towards me. He nodded towards my hand. The broken one.

Instinctually I pulled away. "It's not fixable."

"I still would like to look at it, if I may?" he asked calmly.

I sighed, not happy with his question. "Very well." I put my hand out and he grabbed it gently. He turned it over and ran calloused fingers across it. His hands were extremely warm. The heat was soothing and pleasant on my muscles. They were tense and hard to use now. They were so used to being able to wield a sword and now they could not hold much of anything.

He kept staring at the hand and before I knew it, the heat grew intense, almost unbearable. I said nothing and I didn't move beyond clenching my jaw tightly. As the heat dissipated, he had a strange look on his face. Was that shock or just disappointment that he couldn't fix me?

I spoke softly, I was somewhat saddened he couldn't help me. "I told you it wasn't fixable."

His eyes looked up at my face. "That is not the case, my lady. It is healable, but only by you."

I stared at him in disbelief. "I don't understand. If I could heal it, I would've already."

"I can't say if that is true or not. Is that why you are angry with yourself?"

I took a step away from him. "No."

He gave a small shrug. "I believe you will understand in time what you are capable of."

I blinked a few times, irritated that he felt like I was

able to heal my ruined hand yet had left it in its current state. "I have to ask you a question."

"Ask anything you would like to."

I chewed nervously on my bottom lip, not sure I wanted an honest answer to the question that had plagued me for months. "Why was I unable to heal, to defend myself? In the past, I've always felt the magic there, waiting for me to call for it. When I would, it was taking care of things, protecting me."

He looked like he was choosing his words carefully before saying anything he shouldn't. "It protected you in its own way, kept you alive, but things are different now. You learned who you truly are. You discovered how to use your gift the best you could. Your mark has healed completely, it's no longer broken. When you were relying on your magic, it would come out to do its own bidding as it pleased. You forget the magic that makes you the artifact was once a wild, chaotic, free, untamed beast on its own. It wanted nothing more than to lash out and strike against whoever it could. Now it is contained in a vessel it cannot control and is told to do as its master wishes. When your mark was broken, it was able to be free to unleash itself as it was born to do. It doesn't desire to be tamed or controlled, just be free. However, now that your mark has bound it and chained it back up again, the only way to release it and use it is to understand how to control it."

"So how do I do that? How do I learn to control it?" I asked. I wanted to be strong again, be fixed.

A friendly smile curled up his mouth. "Just ask and we will teach you the best we can given the situation."

I looked down at his hand still touching mine and I whispered the words that I had only told one other.

"Tatiana controlled them, those elementals. I don't want to hurt or kill them, but I don't want them to kill me either."

He nodded, a grimness covering his face. "I understand. I truly do. But that is the decision and the path that they are on. Just as you are on a path that you cannot change."

I kept my eyes downcast. I know they didn't ask to be in the position they were in, but neither did I. I couldn't let them continue unchecked.

He must've sensed my thoughts. "You don't want to hurt them, but you must understand it may come down to you or them. You have the power to win against them. It's there but not in the way you are used to it protecting you. You must protect yourself at all costs."

I looked at my mark, studying the intricate purple lines there. Flesh that once was twisted and marred now had beautiful purple lines running across it. I nodded and looked up at him, determination clear upon my face. "Will you help me? Will you try and show me how to control it, how to fight?"

Masou smiled broadly. "I can do that."

"Then show me what I need to do."

Chapter Eleven

Every single muscle in my body ached in one way or another. I had been training with different Maesters day and night for two weeks without a break. At this time, I wasn't sure what the point of my training was.

I knew I needed it to get stronger and learn about being a Vayu and how the elementals used their powers. But it had begun to take a mental toll on me. The first couple of days had been a struggle I wasn't prepared for. Having them attack me with their abilities, over and over again. It sent memories of my fight with the four elementals shooting straight into my brain. Everything in my mind and body screamed out for the training to stop.

Even in moments of very little sleep, I had woken up in tears, sweat covering my body as the reminders of the past kept coming back to me. The moments in the throne room with Tatiana's cruel face staring down at me, a wicked smile playing on her features as she watched her elementals do her bidding one by one taking their turns to attack me.

The water elemental drowning me repeatedly as I struggled to breathe any air into my lungs. The fire elemental, burning my flesh to a blackened crisp, all the nerves screaming out in excruciating agony. An air elemental pushing me against a wall with extreme force, an invisible weight on my chest as air was siphoned away from me. And the earth elemental, one by one slowly crushing all my bones in my body under the weight of massive rocks.

And I was helpless. Helpless to intervene. Helpless to do anything but stand and watch the grisly scene as I was viciously attacked in a never-ending cycle. The dreams came every single night, without a minute of relief. I didn't know how to let it go. How to move past it. Would I ever?

I wanted so badly to tell myself I could and would. I wanted to believe that it was merely because I lost, and I was a sore loser. But as time went on, I became more and more suspicious that that wasn't the case. It wasn't the fact that I lost. In the end, it was the lack of control.

I had always been able to, for the most part, control my destiny, control what was going on in my life. In that moment in the palace, I was out of control. It felt like there was no way out. I truly was going to die and couldn't prevent it. I didn't like that feeling. The feeling of helplessness. The feeling like no matter what I did I couldn't run away. That they would get me even here in a place far from their reach and if someone so powerful could feel this powerless, I could only imagine how other people in Tileon felt, how helpless they must feel at night. Those were the nagging thoughts and feelings that kept me up most nights.

I stared at the ceiling while stray tears slid down my temple and into my hair. I was trying to control my breathing as it came out in ragged gasps. Humid sticky sweat clung to my body, the heat here was atrocious. The disgusting feeling of being smothered in a hot wetness as the world around me constantly moved. The jungle was always alive, it never truly slept.

I laid there just thinking about everything. About all the training I had finished and how much more I had to do. I was proud of myself for how far I had come. Masou taught me a few healing tricks, just the basics he said. None of which worked when I tried them on my hand, however.

That was a huge disappointment, even if I could heal other people and their ailments, which could come in handy soon. Others taught me not how to attack, not how to fight, but something else I hadn't really learned how to do. Defend myself against attacks.

Even when I was in Heka, I had only been taught how to fight with my magic. I had never been shown how to defend against others. How to ward off an attack from other elementals, especially ones working together. That was the knowledge I truly needed, how to dodge and evade. In all my years of fighting I had never focused on learning the act of evading, it just wasn't who I was. It wasn't my style of fighting, but it needed to be.

The various teachers tried to talk to me about the war. What my plan was when I returned to Tileon. I couldn't give them the answers they wanted. I knew I couldn't go in there, headstrong, trying to take out Tatiana like I did before. No, I wouldn't be able to avoid this war. No matter what I did, it would be her army against any army I could have.

I wasn't thrilled at the prospect of fighting against her. I wasn't happy with the thought of having to come face to face with others like me and fight them. Put them down. Perhaps even kill them. I reminded myself I didn't have a choice in any of this. Not in this war. My near death experience had changed my outlook on death and fighting. I now had a hesitation that previously wasn't there.

Unfortunately, things were as they were. People would die, good people who didn't deserve it, and they would be mourned by their loved ones. This war seemed unavoidable, it was fated to happen and so here I was training my ass off, hoping against hope that I could get strong enough that not many needed to die.

I took another breath. Then another. In and out. I had slowed my heartbeat enough that I didn't feel like I was in the middle of a panic attack. I swung my feet over the edge of the makeshift bed and placed them firmly on the ground. The solid stone beneath my feet held a coolness to it, a welcome relief in this heat. The carefully carved blocks were safe, solid, and steady underneath me. While everything else in the world was shaky.

I walked out of the stone room that I had called home for the past couple of weeks. I moved aside a blanket hanging from the doorway, the only form of privacy I had. With bare feet upon stone, I went left to walk down the hall and past the multitude of rooms full of all kinds of interesting things. Things that you could spend a lifetime sorting through. What information did the scrolls have? What kind of paintings were these? And where did they come from?

I felt pulled towards many of the items, and I realized some of the stuff here had been from previous lives of mine. Those lives felt so far away, yet so close to me. I'm sure if I were to touch the items, memories would pop into my mind. I didn't need any of my past lives in my mind right now. So, I walked past them not wanting to see any other reminders of my past. I didn't want to know about those lifetimes. Not when this one was so close to my heart.

Step by step I continued, down the stone stairs and into the dirt of the jungle. Moistness accompanied it, along with what felt like moss. I walked through the trees, stepping carefully around anything alive. My hand was aflame with magic to light my way in the darkness.

After a few long minutes, I came to a stop in front of the large staircase leading up to another pyramid-like structure. This one housed the white drakyn from Kaia's dreams. I hadn't brought myself to go in there yet, I didn't dare. Instead, I sat on the steps every night, asking myself if it was time to enter. Was I ready to? I didn't know if I was. The drakyn told me not to come back until I had accepted who I was.

I didn't want to go in there and be turned away again. So here I waited every single night on the steps for the moment I was ready. I couldn't decide whether I knew it was time or not. I watched the sunrise peak above the tree canopy once more, the blues and purples of night turned into bright pinks and oranges. I enjoyed each one I was able to watch.

Was I hiding here in Arcadia? Was I hiding away from what Tileon held? I wasn't quite sure anymore. My thoughts were interrupted by Masou.

"Good morning," he said in a rather chipper voice.

"Morning," I replied with a small smile.

He sat down next to me. "I would ask how things are going, but we both know the answer to that question. Don't we?"

I gave a weak shrug. "Do we?"

"Well, you come here every single morning and sit upon these steps in the exact same spot, but you never go any higher." He gave me a knowing look.

I shifted, uncomfortable that he noticed my nightly habit. "I'm not ready to go in yet."

He stared at me, his eyes doing all the talking.

I felt the need to defend myself. "I'm not prepared fully. I need more time and more training."

He placed his elbows on his knees and leaned forward holding both hands together. "How much more time?"

"I don't know. As long as it takes, I guess."

He sighed. "I was afraid you'd say that."

"Why?"

His response caught me off guard. "You can't keep staying here."

I swallowed back angry words. "Are you telling us to leave?"

He shook his head. "No, of course not. You're welcome in Arcadia for as long as you desire. Yet I must be honest with you. I feel as if you are trying to avoid certain responsibilities you have by staying here."

I did not like that he seemed to have read my mind. The words popped out in a defensive tone. "I'm not avoiding anything."

He chuckled wryly. "Let's try to be honest with each other, yes?"

I didn't respond.

He took my silence as a yes apparently. "You are ready. Ready to go up those steps and face what you are hiding from. You are choosing not to. As I said, you may stay here for as long as you truly wish to do so, but you must know in your heart that you cannot stay here forever. Tileon still needs you, it has already fallen into chaos and darkness.

Every day more and more innocent lives suffer. I understand you are scared of what is to come, you're not used to this kind of life."

I bitterly answered. "The life of a hero? No, not really."

He grinned. "No, not the life of a hero. In a way, that you are accustomed to."

I stared at him. "Then what do you mean?"

"The life of uncertainty. I know your story to a point. Where you were when Marcus found you? That life was certain, predictable. Every night the same thing, every day the same thing. You fought, you would win. Earn money for your master. Eat, drink, and go about daily existence. Make weapons and make friends. A simple life every single day, it was the exact same until it wasn't anymore. You knew who you were. At least you thought you did, and then one day it was ripped from you. Along came someone out of nowhere that made you question everything you ever knew about yourself. Who is Niya? I bet if I asked you that question then, it would be such a different answer than if I asked now."

I stared down to the ground that was starting to fill with early mornings light. "You're right. Back then I would have told you I was a slave."

He scoffed. "Hardly."

I gave him a dirty look. "I don't understand."

"You would have answered that you were the undefeated champion of the Swords and Sin. That you were the best blacksmith to ever live. You had an abundance of pride for who you were."

"I was those things," I said quietly.

"You are still that person. You just have a longer story now. Yet who you are now is unclear to you. Who is Niya now?"

I shook my head, trying to shake away the rush of emotions. "She is a coward. She's filled with doubts and fears. I'm scared to face Tatiana, that if I do, I won't scrape by barely alive, I'll die. I'm afraid that I'll never, ever defeat her. I've been told I'm this powerful artifact of the Vayu, that I'm the Savior of Tileon. That I'm all these amazing things." I say the next words as a whisper. "I don't feel like that at all. Not anymore."

He smiled. "You felt untouchable? Invincible in a way. Thought that your power would protect you no matter what."

"Well, it didn't. It failed me when I needed it most, it was not there," I spat the words out.

"Not because it wasn't there. Because you needed to be reminded of something very important."

"Yeah, what's that? How to die?"

He laughed. "No, that you're still human. Underneath the power is a real person. You are not indestructible. No matter how much you wish to be. You are still flesh and bone. One day, you will pass from this existence. Your soul will go wherever souls go. And then it will be born again like it always is. Until then, you are in this body, a body that you know can still be broken."

"Trust me, I learned that lesson."

"It was a good reminder."

"A good reminder?" I asked.

"Yes. You have weaknesses. You're not all powerful. You're not all seeing. I think understanding one's weakness is the best way to understand how to be powerful."

I played with my hands. I'd never given it much thought that while I may be incredibly powerful, I was also weak. Flesh and bones were so easy to harm.

Masou continued speaking. "Tatiana feels the same

way about herself as you feel about yourself. She is extremely powerful in a different way than you are. Who could question her, who could topple her from the throne she sits firmly on? Perhaps you need to remind her that she is also human. Those made of flesh and bone can die. That is a sad part of our reality. Are you afraid of death?"

"No," I answered immediately, but that was a lie. I couldn't look him in the eye when I spoke the truth out loud. "I didn't used to be. It seemed like some far off concept. Something I would have to deal with when I was eighty years old. Or one day there would be an accident in the fighting pits. A knife would go where it wasn't supposed to. It's different, you know, being stabbed with a knife. Usually it's quick, even painless. Not like…" Flashes of the throne room came to mind, it haunted all of the nightmares that continued to plague me nightly. "Not like other deaths that are drawn out, full of pain and unbelievable suffering. I don't want to be in pain at the end."

He nodded. "I understand. I do." He paused, his face taking on a mask of concern. "You should know something."

I turned to meet his eyes. "Yes?"

"I don't know how to say it, so forgive my bluntness. Typically, elementals, especially Vayu, that are powerful and know how to fully use their gifts, can live a very long time. Some extend their life well beyond centuries."

I nodded. I'd heard of such abilities and seen it with my own eyes. Ademar was extremely old but looked middle aged, and James the ship captain had alluded to being older than he appeared to be. "Yes, I know. I'm not sure how they do it, but I've seen a few that were a lot older than their true age."

"I have extended my lifespan a few times as well.

Because of who you are..." He sputtered, trying to get the words out. "You should also have such a gift and ability to make your life longer should you desire it to be."

I scrunched my eyebrows together. The thought had never occurred to me that I could live so long. Live to be a hundred or maybe even as old as Ademar, but then his next words stopped me in my tracks.

"Usually those that are strong and powerful have this gift. When your mark was cut from you, your gift was blocked. It was hidden from your knowledge and only used at times when you were afraid. It lashed out uncontrollably in mass waves of pure undiluted power. Because of that, the power that you have used has drained your life greatly. It burned out how long you would live. You will not live to be as old as you should. After feeling your life-force when I tried to heal you, I'm afraid, in this life at least, you will have an early death my lady."

I stared at him. Not blinking, not moving. Every muscle in my body froze. Not even my breath came out. My heart, however, raced, thundering violently in my ears. I bit my lip. *Fuck.* "How long do I have?" The words barely came out.

His voice was soft and soothing. His face was sad. "It's hard to say truly. If I were to give an estimate, I'd say maybe a couple years longer."

My eyes filled with tears. "So, I won't be able to win this war."

He shook his head slightly. "You will. That is why you will only have a couple more years. If you do not fight... perhaps another decade. We both know you will end up fighting. That you will go against Tatiana, against Pyron. You will use that magic to save those people and using that much magic will burn you out even more. I'm afraid that this war ultimately will lead to your death in a round-about sort of way."

I laughed bitterly. "No matter the outcome, Pyron will take my life."

"If you wish to see it that way."

"Well," I stood up suddenly, "I already feel dead inside. How much worse could it get?" I turned around and began walking up the stone steps. I'd never truly feel ready, but I was sick of waiting. I was tired. So, fucking tired of questioning everything. I knew what to do. Who I needed to speak with.

I walked down the dark hall alone and there, at the end, was the entrance to the tunnel that would lead me to the underground cavern. I once again tumbled down the stone chute full of cobwebs and dirt. They flew into my face, and I was ejected into a heap at the bottom.

The darkness was all encompassing. I looked around stupidly hoping to see some kind of flicker of something, anything besides the empty void. There in the distance, the light of blue orbs started shining. I watched as two blue slitted eyes stared at me.

I could tell in the dark she had her head cocked as she stared down at me.

"*You came back*," the magical woman-like voice said.

"Hello Aleera."

" *It seems you finally remembered,*" she replied with a happy tone.

I nodded in the darkness, not really knowing whether she could see the movement or not. "I did."

"*Is that why you've come back?*"

"You told me to return once I had embraced who or rather what I was. I've done that, for the most part." I hadn't completely accepted that being the artifact would ultimately cost me my life. The thought hadn't sunk in, yet.

The two glowing blue eyes came closer to me. Fires sprang up along the cavern once more, pitching the cave into a mysterious orange light. "*Yes, you have. It appears the path was not easy.*"

"No, it wasn't," I replied coldly.

"*Would you like to talk about it?*"

I shook my head. I didn't have time to discuss my feelings, I had a war to fight. "What's there to talk about? You told me to return once I had embraced being the artifact and I've done that."

"*Yes, you have. Do you understand everything that entails?*" she asked carefully.

My voice held an edge to it. "You mean the fact that I won't live a long, normal life?"

She bowed her head in remorse. "*Not this time, I'm afraid.*"

I nodded, tears welling in my eyes. "Well, it is what it is." I tried to get my emotions under control, but she said something that I needed to hear.

"*Stop pushing them down, my dear Niya and let them out. There's no one else here but me, and I understand what you're feeling. All that you've had to give up. All that you've lost. Most would have abandoned this path a long time ago. They would have stayed in a city full of magic, whether it was sleeping or not, and turned a blind eye to all the wretched things around them. Or perhaps they would have even taken up a handsome sea captain's offer to explore the world and left behind any commitments. You'd be able to do as you desired, however you wished to do it. But you stayed on your path.*"

I sat down on the floor abruptly with my back against the rough stone wall. "I wanted to. I thought about it every day. Where I would live. How I would eat. How I could survive." I played with my finger. "I thought about all of it and then I felt guilty for even considering it."

"*You should not feel guilty for having basic emotions and fears. It's a normal human reaction.*"

I whispered, "But I did. Felt like I was no better than Tatiana for even thinking about abandoning those people."

The drakyn knelt down as best she could with her massive body. Her face was only a couple feet from where I sat. "*I have lived a long life. Spent many of them with you in fact. I've seen the absolute worst of humanity. Trust me when I tell you, you're not one of them. Thinking of freedom, of being*" safe and secure, not worrying about sacrificing peace or people dying. Who wouldn't want to be rid of such things? War is messy. I've seen plenty of it, as have you. It's not some simple thing where you can just go into it hoping for the best. No, it's a brutal thing. The hardest part is knowing that so many will not make it to the end."

I bit my lower lip. "How do you look them in the eye and tell them it's for the good of everyone?"

Aleera sighed, causing the ground to rumble slightly. "You do it if it's what you believe to be true. But that's not the only thing that bothers you, you're also afraid of making a mistake."

I shifted uncomfortably. "I made a mistake once."

"Yes, you did, but you didn't cost anybody their lives. You only risked your own."

I huffed. "Not this time. What about next time? What if next time I cost someone their life? What if next time, people get hurt?"

"They will get hurt. You can't think about next time, just what's happening now. You are a warrior and a leader. People will die during this war and if you desire someone to blame or point fingers at, and you choose you, so be it. But you must understand it's okay to sacrifice a few for the good of the many. Particularly if it means a better future."

"I'm not ready for it," I said weakly.

"You are as ready as one could be. What do you think holds you back?"

I shrugged.

"You're afraid of getting hurt."

The side of my lip turned up in disdain. "So, they keep telling me."

"You don't have to be." She stood up on her legs. Her full height almost scraping the top of the ginormous cavern. She dipped her head down, her face coming close to mine.

I peered up at her through my lashes, wide eyed at her how marvelous she was.

"This time you won't be fighting against Tatiana alone. We will do it together, as one."

Her head touched mine and once again there was an explosion of power shared between us. It wasn't like the first time, it wasn't painful. I didn't feel searing agony ripping through my body. This time it was like somebody was opening up everything in front of me. She and I were one. She was me and I was her. I could feel all our lives spent together, a warrior and her drakyn flying into battle on so many occasions.

In that moment I knew what we had to do. It wouldn't be pretty, but war never was. I stood up and put my hand on her snout, gently caressing the rough scales. They shimmered brilliantly in the fire light. "I'm ready."

If drakyns could smile, she would be doing so. *"Good. Then there's no need for me to stay here any longer."*

I stared at where I remembered the door to be and then looked back at her. "I don't know exactly how to say this, but I don't think you're fitting out the door."

She tilted her head. *"Well, who said anything about going out through the door?"* She turned around, stared up to the ceiling, and roared loudly.

All the air in the cavern began to heat up. As the heat grew more intense sweat poured down my skin. The fires lining the cavern grew brighter and brighter. I shielded my eyes with my hand and then watched as a massive fire ball launched from her mouth. It hit the very top of the cavern causing rocks to rain down on me and a tiny ray of sunlight to shine through.

She paused for a second to turn her head towards me. *"You may take the door."*

The door that appeared hidden opened wide and I ran, not wanting to get crushed by the rocks that fell in every direction. I darted the best I could to the relative safety of the stone doorway. I made it outside and stood near the tree line of the jungle. I could see the small opening Aleera had made in the side of the temple. Another fire ball blast hit, and stone spewed everywhere. I was thrown off balance as the very ground beneath my feet started to shake in increasing waves. My feet trembled as the dirt floor stirred violently.

It wasn't an earthquake, it was Aleera getting out from the cavern. Two giant white wings popped out from the hole that had been made. She crawled out, dragging her talons into the sides of the stone and releasing herself from the cavern. She spread her wings wide and shook her body, dirt and debris flew everywhere, spraying the forest with the bits of earth. She looked up into the sky at the sun and closed her eyes, basking in its warmth.

I had only seen her deep within the cavern's dim darkness and while I had prior memories of her from old lives, it was nothing like viewing her in person. I'd never witnessed a more glorious sight. The brilliant light of the sun sparkled off her iridescent scales, making her look almost like a rainbow, all the colors blending together in an eye-catching display.

I was rooted to my spot, just watching her standing idly on the now broken temple. I hardly noticed that the Maesters, Theo, and Marcus had come up behind me. They were observing Aleera in both amazement and concern.

For the first time, I heard the old advisor curse under his breath "Shit! Where did that come from?"

I grinned wickedly. "Say hello to Aleera."

I could feel his eyes on me, just as Marcus's were. "You know her?" Theo sputtered out.

"What do you think I came here for? Masou's lessons?" I said sarcastically.

Marcus's voice came out shaky. "This is what you came here for? A fucking drakyn?"

I smiled, proud to call Aleera my bond mate. "Yes. What better thing to use against Tatiana?"

Theo sucked in a breath through his teeth. "Well, I'm sure she'll be surprised."

"I know I am," Marcus said quietly.

"Now what?" Theo asked me.

"Now we go to war." I was ready for a rematch with the four elementals.

He swallowed awkwardly. "That's not what I meant."

I raised an eyebrow at him, with a questioning look.

"I don't know if you've noticed, but I don't think she's going to fit back through the archway we came in or in the hallway and up the stairs, or out the door into the ruins."

I stared at him blankly. *Stupid idiot.* I never thought about how I would get her to Tileon. Theo was right, she would never fit through the doorway.

I heard her voice rumble in my mind. It was an unfamiliar sensation. I felt more than heard her words in my mind as they traveled along our bond. *"We're not going through the archway."*

"I don't understand," I spoke out loud, much to Theo and Marcus's confusion.

"You will." Then she released a roar that disturbed the entire jungle. Birds soared into the air in a frenzy. I covered

my ears with my hands in a useless attempt to prevent anymore ringing in my ears. I did not expect the roars of other drakyns in the distance to answer Aleera.

I studied the other structures and it had never occurred to me that they too could hold a cavern with drakyns as well.

I glanced back at Masou. "How many are there?" I asked.

He shook his head. "I'm not sure. To be honest, the only temple we've ever gone inside is the one with the weapons and other items stored in it. We've obviously tried to explore them, gone up the stairs and down the hallways but never any farther than that. We had read scrolls that mentioned the possibility of drakyns beneath the temples hundreds of years ago. I had no idea that there were still drakyns alive here."

In the far distance, more and more roars rang out. There had to be dozens of them. If they were anything like Aleera...well, I liked our odds. Soon the ground began shaking as the other drakyns broke free of their prisons.

They launched themselves high into the air. Dozens and dozens of drakyns of all sizes and colors flew into the sky. Some were as large as horses, others were larger than a ship. Oranges, reds, greens, and any other color you could think of made up the variety of scales I could see.

They flew around excitedly, testing their unused wings against the wind and their newly discovered freedom. Behind the pyramid-like structure two smaller drakyns landed, one an ocean blue and the other a sunset orange. Aleera crawled down from the temple.

"It's time."

I was confused. "Time for what?" I asked.

"It is time to do what must be done. Are you ready?" she implored.

"I…yes," I responded.

"Good. These two have offered to fly your friends."

My eyebrows went up. "Fly?"

She nodded her head. *"Yes, we are going to fly to Tileon, of course. Do you know of another way to get there?"*

I was left speechless. My mind spun, flying. We would actually travel on drakyns. I turned to Masou. "It seems our time together has come to an abrupt end."

He stared at Aleera, then at me. "Hardly, my lady. We are joining you."

I blinked rapidly. "What?"

"We have been waiting for someone worthy to follow and we've seen all that you have accomplished. We also know what's happened in Tileon. The Maesters are meant to help keep balance in our world. We are not going to sit idly by while you wage this war alone. We will meet you on the other side and try to gather others to our cause."

I gave him a genuine smile. "Thank you Masou for everything, truly." I shook his hand.

"We will see each other soon." He shook the hands of Marcus and Theo as they said their goodbyes.

"Come along." I gestured for the two men to follow me. We walked to the back side of the pyramid-like structure.

"I have never flown before," Marcus squeaked out when he saw the two drakyns waiting to carry him and Theo home.

I gave him a look. "And you think I have? I don't know about any of this. You're supposed to be a king, are you not? This will be easier than fighting against Tatiana and her army."

"If you say so."

"I do," I said firmly. I nodded towards the two drakyns.

The men reluctantly went to them and crawled onto their backs—Marcus on the orange and Theo on the blue. They both looked unsure sitting on top of the scaled creatures.

I giggled at their uncomfortableness and how stiff they sat. "You get to ride ancient drakyns. What are you so afraid of?"

Marcus glared at me. "Falling off."

"Well hold on tight then. Pretend you're riding a horse."

They both tightened their grips on the large beasts. Aleera bent down in a crouch, giving me the opportunity to get onto her back. I crawled up her leg clumsily and onto her neck. I was higher up than I expected to be.

She glanced back at me with one of her eyes. *"You should hold on. We're not going to be going slow."*

I clutched onto her neck, holding on to the glistening scales. "I'm ready Aleera." I glanced over at my companions, terror evident on their faces. I understood their fear, this was a new experience. One that could end in disaster.

Aleera's body tensed, her muscles coiled tightly beneath me before she launched us into the air with all her energy. My body, especially my stomach, hadn't caught up to my head as she propelled herself into the air. My stomach dropped into a pit as we quickly ascended into the sky.

While it was exhilarating and knocked the breath out of my lungs, I could hear screaming, and I wasn't sure if it was from Theo or Marcus, or maybe both. Powerful wings beat through the wind, slicing cleanly through the air.

I turned my head to catch a glimpse of the ground, still clutching onto Aleera for dear life. I could see the jungle land of Arcadia below us. It stretched out far into the distance and was speckled with countless pyramids.

From this height, I couldn't see the archway home or the Maesters. I turned my head to see behind us and accompanying us in the sky were thirty to forty beautiful jewel-colored drakyns. They beat their wings in a steady rhythm and flew around us.

I could hear the buzz of their minds within my head. Some were bloodthirsty, but they were at least all coherent. It wasn't like the minds of the drakyns I encountered in Pyron. When I pushed them to attack their masters, they were mere primal animals. They had no conscious thoughts besides their owners' commands and the desire for bloodshed. These drakyns were different, intelligent. I could feel how old they were. How sentient they were. They were alive with power pulsing beneath their scales. They knew exactly what they wanted and what to do. They understood that Aleera was in charge. They were ready to fight. They had been cooped up for so long and they were enjoying their freedom.

It wasn't long until we were flying over crystal blue water. I yelled over the wind, hoping Aleera could hear me. "Are you trying to tell me that Tileon is on the same world as Arcadia."

I could hear Aleera's answer within my mind. *"Yes. All the doors in the place you call the Hall of Doors are connected to this world. Different places and different lands are not explored by many. Knowledge of them has been misplaced for quite some time."*

I internally started counting how many doors were in that hall? Was it sixteen? "I had no idea."

"You'd be surprised how small your land is. But that doesn't mean it's not worth fighting for."

My curiosity grew. I wanted to see these other lands, know about them. "Well, perhaps we will get to see more of the world after Tileon is saved."

"Perhaps. Until then, enjoy the view."

My courage spiked and I slowly sat up. I held on with my thighs and my hands. The wind whipped through my hair. I closed my eyes and enjoyed the feeling of sun upon my skin as I rode on the back of the drakyn bonded to me.

Daylight faded in to night as we flew towards Tileon. The constant beating of Aleera's wings made me drowsy. I tried to keep myself awake—I was afraid that if I fell asleep it'd be a long drop into the ocean, and it would be the unfortunate end to this life.

Theo and Marcus also tried to keep themselves awake. As we flew on for such a long period of time, I wasn't sure how long it would take for us to get back to our land. It was crazy to think that we lived on a small piece of land, that it wasn't the whole entirety of this world, that there were other places ripe to explore.

I thought back to James. He knew about them. He had told me that we could leave Tileon and go somewhere else. Places that were safe. I wondered if he knew about Arcadia. Or if perhaps there were other lands he had spoken of.

As dawn began to break, the pink hues of daylight pushed away the midnight blues. Theo and Marcus's drakyns flew closer to Aleera.

Marcus shouted as loud as he could. "How much longer?"

Aleera's voice sounded in my mind. *"A few more hours*

and we will arrive. When the sun is at its highest point towards noon, we will arrive in the Old Forest."

I looked to the two men and tried to scream back. Hoping my voice carried over the gushing wind. "We will land in the Old Forest in a few hours. Then you need to make sure that our army is ready. It's time for us to fight. This is our one and only opportunity. I don't think we'll get another."

They both nodded their understanding.

Theo yelled over the rushing air, "You wouldn't happen to have the ability to send a letter, would you?"

I scrunched up my eyebrows. "Why? What did you have in mind?"

Today felt different.

It felt like something was coming, that it was just around the corner. I didn't always question my sanity, but at times like this I couldn't help doing so. With a daughter like mine, it was hard not to. I had learned a long time ago to not question things.

How little things made the biggest difference in life. How many things, choices, and random events had led me to be here. To be in a sewer full of shit, puke, and who knew what else. A once great king brought to his ultimate low point.

I laid on my back on my shitty little cot—my own little slice of paradise. I heard tiny wings flapping, something odd to hear in this horrible place. I sat up and looked around, trying to find the cause of the sound. There, flying around the ceiling, was a strange looking bird. It was the size of my hand and bright yellow with streaks of red and white on its chest.

It dove towards me, curiosity and fear making my heart race. It dropped something at my feet and flew off. I stared at where it disappeared, baffled at its sudden arrival and departure.

I picked up what it had let fall on my bed. It was a small, rolled up piece of paper. I unrolled it gently and held the paper up to a nearby flame. It held barely legible writing. The messy words said:

It's time to be free from Pyron. Gather everyone you can and meet us in the Old Forest as soon as you are able to.

I cocked my eyebrow and whispered to myself, "Finally, something interesting. It's about damn time."

Chapter Thirteen

It took about three days to reach the Old Forest by drakyn. It seemed like barely any time had passed, and I was convinced they used magic to accomplish such a task. It was strange how amazing it felt to be riding on the back of a drakyn—how *right* it felt.

I tried to figure out the direction in which we were heading, and it appeared that we were going towards the northwest to get to Tileon. I had perused all the books in the library at Heka when I was researching the artifact. I'd never seen any mention of lands other than Tileon. I didn't recall seeing any information on the arches or the Hall of Doors, especially that they took you to other lands upon our world.

Somewhere out there were other places in our world, places that had barely been explored or spoken of. The thought filled me with curiosity and wonder, but it also raised so many questions. Where were they? How big were they? Who lived there? If anyone? Were there other drakyns? Other people like me? Elementals living in peace, or was the world something else entirely?

Perhaps the people in Heka didn't know any of those answers or they knew a long time ago and chose to forget, for one reason or another. Ademar had told me that he didn't know anything about the various doors and rooms. He had only heard rumors about where the one door led. That it was supposedly filled with people on the other side that were dangerous, dark, evil, and murderous. Which is why the door had been bricked over eventually.

But it wasn't a bad place, it was Arcadia. A jungle land filled with giant pyramid-like structures, filled with drakyns that were so old, time didn't even have meaning to some of them.

This whole time I could have gone there. Could have trained with the Maesters sooner, met Aleera with Alec. It was interesting how the magic dissuaded you from entering the room and going through the arch. They probably didn't want anyone powerful to find out about the secrets that lay on the other side. Maesters were crafty, I suppose, in that way. I respected their secrecy. They hid themselves so well, I hadn't spotted them on my first trip to Arcadia.

My thoughts moved from Arcadia back to Tileon. I had to admit, I was nervous to land in the ruins of the Old Forest. How many people would come to our cause? How many people would be there when we finally landed? Hundreds, thousands, or just a mere dozen? Or perhaps none at all?

I noticed something different about my feelings this time. I wasn't scared. I wasn't shaking and filled with dread. While I was nervous about what was to come, I wasn't scared out of my mind to face Tatiana again. No, this time I felt a thrill go through me, adrenaline spiking within me. I recognized the feeling, I used to experience it right before I would enter into the pits and face an oppo-nent. Somehow I knew deep in my heart that I would beat Tatiana.

The words Masou told me were still fresh, swirling around in my mind. No matter what I did, whether I fought or didn't fight, I wasn't long for this world. At this point, truly what did it matter whether I hid myself away or stepped up? I'd always told myself I would die fighting and now was the time to put that to the test.

I was ready and I hoped the others were willing to fight with me. I prayed to everything that I knew, to the power that made me who I am, what I am, that I would find other people waiting for us in the Old Forest. Marcus was confident that there would be thousands of people waiting for us. That he knew many would want to fight for their chance at freedom.

Ones who were sick of being put down by Tatiana. But I wondered if that was true, or if he was just hoping for the best. I remembered during Caleb's time, how many people wanted freedom and yet, so few chose to fight. Fear was a strong emotion and even stronger motivator.

Tatiana had put terror into the heart of so many. I wouldn't blame them for not coming forward. I didn't even blame them if they chose to hide. I couldn't say that I hadn't felt the same way at times—especially when I was lying half dead in the cabin on the Mischief. I had wanted to hide away there forever. Pretend like the outside world didn't exist.

That was my reality. I knew that with or without all the extra people, we would fight. I would fight until my dying breath to free Tileon. It's what I was made to do, and I would do it with pride.

I steadied myself as land came into view and I realized

where we were—what land I was now watching grow larger by the minute.

I looked over to Marcus and Theo and whispered to myself, knowing they couldn't hear me over the wind, "Welcome home to Azzaria."

Aleera swooped around to go up the coast. Far off in the distance you could see it: the rocky cliff side that turned flat for the palace that resided on top of it. I couldn't see the city beyond it, only the sun shining off the numerous windows. Aleera didn't get close enough to where it would become an issue. She didn't want us to be seen before we needed to be.

We were too far away for Tatiana to notice us, hopefully. We were heading north along the coast of Azzaria until we could no longer go without being seen. We swept around far left, the air becoming colder and colder. A chill settled into my bones.

We drew close to the land of Aquaen or what little remained of it. I watched closely as we flew past it, this was the first time I'd ever seen it. It was burnt pieces of wood and ash. Only small glaciers remained as we flew pass Ahuan, the once proud capital, with an ice palace that I would never in this lifetime get to see. We went between the largest of the Aquaenian islands and a smaller one, then flew straight down into the heart of the Old Forest.

As we got closer to the ruins, I saw specks on the ground. No, not specks. People. There were actually people here! This was amazing. This meant that there were others willing to join us. Help us, fight with us. Others who felt what we felt about the current issues in Tileon.

Then I saw something I wasn't expecting to see. Or perhaps I should have. They were not far off the coast. It was a ship, a ship I recognized well. A huge grin split my face. It was the Mischief, which meant that James was here, and then I noticed other ships were sailing this way.

He had found other captains who were willing to fight and were willing to use their vessels to help. We would need ships willing to go up against Tatiana's. I was beyond grateful for his help.

We flew lower towards the ruins. Onlookers stared up at us, their mouths agape. As we swooped in, they quickly moved out of the way, making space for us as we came in for a landing. Aleera needed the most room for her massive body, and she flew towards the back of the ruins, where no one was.

Marcus and Theo landed closer to the potential army. I carefully made my way off Aleera. I patted her neck, feeling the rough but hard scales underneath my hand.

"Thank you," I said weakly. My legs were wobbly from riding on her back for so long.

She dipped her head regally. *"If you don't mind, I will do a little hunting. I'm very hungry and I need the strength."*

I instantly nodded. "Of course."

"I also need one other thing."

I was confused. "Such as?"

She lifted her head into the air and opened her mouth. She let out her mighty roar into the sky. Off in the distance, we heard her call answered dozens of times. It sent a shiver down my spine.

I glanced around at the other people; they shared faces of amusement, excitement, and pure terror. Drakyns had been used for so many years against us by Pyron. To hurt us and kill us. Here we were using them for our good. It was time to even the playing field. To push Tatiana back into Pyron and fix everything or die trying.

I walked over to join Theo and Marcus, and there I

spotted a familiar grin accompanied by a familiar swagger. I don't know what came over me, but I ran over and hugged the giant pirate. He took a step back, most likely not expecting the sign of affection.

He chuckled happily. "So that's what it takes to get a hug from you."

I released him from the embrace and stepped back to look up at his face. "I'm just glad to see you here in one piece."

He grinned. "I gave you my word that I would be here."

"I know, but I didn't think you'd follow through. Where did you find all these people?"

"Of course I'd follow through, I always keep my word, especially to a beautiful woman. They were hiding in different places that few knew about. They were more than willing to come to our aid."

I cocked my head. "You mean to your aid?"

He shook his head. "No, to ours. They want to fight for you."

My eyes went wide. "I'm sorry, what?"

"They want to fight for you."

"Why me?" I asked.

"Are you truly shocked? Why not you?"

I tried to find the right words. "I'm just…"

He glanced around, making sure nobody could overhear us, and gently pulled me off to the side. "I know I haven't seen you in a while and it's not my place. But you need to remind yourself of something important."

"Which would be?" I said with a lowered voice.

"That, technically, for all intents and purposes, you are a queen of Azzaria and princess of Mageia, whatever that entails. You are also an extremely powerful elemental.

We've seen your power, your gift. So, it wasn't good one time, that doesn't mean it's never going to be good. They follow you because you are a leader. Marcus hid in a sewer for the last five years, never once seeing if there was anybody out there that needed help. No, instead, he just didn't care. You risked your life for that woman in the town square. They know about that, know how much you risked doing that. While they may not know how hard it was for you to come back from that, they see your strength. Besides, you just rode in on a fucking drakyn. They will follow you in this fight. Not Marcus. Not Tatiana. No one else but you."

I looked at him with concern. "I can't say that I totally agree with that. I understand it to a point, and if they're willing to take orders, then so be it."

"Good evening!" He turned around and began yelling to get everyone's attention. All their eyes focused on the large pirate, but I noticed they darted towards me every couple of minutes.

"What are you doing?" I hissed under my breath.

He glanced back at me with a sly grin but didn't utter a word in my direction.

I looked off into the large crowd of people from all over Tileon and there I spotted Marcus with a blonde woman standing next to him. Annabelle. I was surprised to see her here in the Old Forest but before I could think more about it, James started barking out a speech.

"Fellow friends and family. I know you are tired. Hungry. Scared. I know the feeling. It's been a frightening, horrifying couple of years that we have endured. Been made to struggle through. Try and do our absolute best with what little we have available to us. I am beyond grateful to see you here standing with us. As we make history here today. It is time to push back against Pyron, to fight back against those that would oppress us. It's past time to get rid of Tatiana. To fight her for what she has done to not only Tileon but to those that we love, have lost, and so many other grievances. Because of that, because I believe in this fight, in this cause, I follow the one and only queen that I recognize. Niya." He grabbed me by the shoulders and pushed me in front of him.

My eyes widened for a moment and words failed me. Then I felt his rough calloused hand in mine as he knelt down before me. I watched as sea blue eyes danced with mischief, and a hint of something else, as he placed a kiss upon my hand.

He got up, bowed deeply, and moved aside. Soon others came to stand before me, each bowing down, each giving me some moniker that they felt best suited me. The Maesters, when it was their turn, spoke in the language that I didn't recognize before, but I now knew was a language that was spoken a long time ago, during my first life.

In that language, which pulled memories from the past, they honored me for being a true Vayu, for being the artifact, and bringing balance back to a world that had been overrun with chaos. I was honored by all their love, devotion, and willingness to do what needed to be done.

I looked around at the hundreds of people gathered and spoke in a loud steady voice. "I want to thank each and every one of you for your bravery. I know how much fear you must all have right now as I share it. I understand how much of a sacrifice it is to be here. How much so many of you have lost, your homes, lands. Your brothers, sisters, mothers, fathers, and children. I can't even begin to imagine how much devastation and suffering you've had to endure over these last five years. But no more! No more blood will be spilled endlessly for one woman's conquest for power. No longer will our lands burn. No, Pyron will go back to their borders. They will learn to respect Tileon and who we are. No longer will we have to tolerate a tyrant!"

Before the next motivational words could be spoken, one of the crewmen from the Mischief came sprinting up to James and whispered something in his ear. He looked at the man with shock evident in his eyes, and his face turned white.

He took a few steps toward me and his hot breath caressed my ear as his lips moved. He whispered words that made my heart race. "Tatiana flies this way on her drakyn. Her army is at her back. They just entered the border of the Old Forest."

I glanced at him and nodded. I faced back toward the crowd. "Tatiana is on her way here with her army. I know this is ahead of the expected time we thought we had." I watched as people murmured to each other. Fear leaked onto their features and the energy changed. "Please do not be afraid. We will win this war, we have just cause, and I promise you I will do everything within my power to stop her even if it costs me my last breath."

I watched as their faces turned hopeful and I smiled. "It's time to prepare for one final war. Blood will be spilled, I guarantee you that, and I know it will be Tatiana's."

Fresh, salty ocean air blew through the open windows, causing the sheer curtains to rustle in the cool night breeze. It was such a peaceful calming experience. I lied there watching them blow in and out slowly. As I lied in bliss, I smiled to myself. I had everything I'd ever wanted, everything I had ever needed.

My father had held me back for so long. A part of me wished he was here. To see this. To see how great I had made Pyron. I took it from a laughing joke, something people would whisper about, to hate on, and discuss as one would walk by. No longer. They were afraid to even utter the word in any form of disrespect.

They grew to respect our might and power, *my* power. I had been afraid that I could lose it, the power I had built up for years. That girl, she had given me cause for concern. I laughed into the dark and silent room. She fell so easily, toppled over like a baby being pushed to the ground.

I must say I was disappointed that I was forced to punish those four. They had failed me in their duties, I wanted them to kill her. Remove her from any questions that could be asked. It would have been wonderful to see her head upon the gates. Who would dare question me then? No one. They would have feared it too much.

Instead, she got away, not even my drakyn could catch her. She was gone as far as the reports stated. If the long fall from the cliff didn't kill her, the blood loss must've. I admit I had sent out two ships and drakyns to search the water for her body, and I was assured that the water had claimed her.

She was the last of my concerns, I had no worries anymore. I was safe. There was no way any form of rebellion could continue. Not now. Any chance they may have had died with her. I don't know why, but anger rose inside me. Her voice echoed in a mocking tone in my mind. *You're not the queen. I am. I will always be the true queen.*

I sat up quickly, my pulse beating fast, gritting my teeth together, and I said to no one, merely the breezy air, "I am the queen. Me, Tatiana. Not just the queen of Pyron, of Keme, of Azzaria. No, I am the queen of Tileon. I always will be, my children will be after me."

I smiled smugly as I placed my feet upon the floor, a sudden thirst pulling me from my cozy comfort. I strolled barefoot out of my room, navigating the hallways easily as I walked to the kitchen for some fresh water. On my way there I passed by the hallway that led to the council chambers where I noticed a flickering light. Someone was awake and sitting in the council room late at night.

Odd. I stopped in my tracks, staring in the direction I was heading but my eyes flickered back to the cracked door with candlelight spilling out. I turned on my heels and changed course. My thoughts of water to quench my thirst were forgotten as I got closer and closer to the chamber room door.

Voices drifted out to me, hushed but clearly upset. I narrowed my eyes, preparing myself as I entered the room to see two people inside. They quickly stopped talking and bowed to the floor.

"My queen," they said in unison.

"What is going on?" I asked.

They glanced between each other nervously but said nothing.

My voice turned frosty. "I asked a question. I expect an answer."

The scrawny little man on the left looked around nervously. "We received some news."

A cruel smile split my face. "About what?" I again

looked at both of them as they twitched about uncomfortably.

The robust man on the right spoke this time. "It's about the Old Forest."

I was growing impatient. "What about it?"

"We've received word that there is an army gathering there."

I arched my eyebrow. "Really?"

"Yes, my lady."

"Whose army? Who would dare to gather such an army?" I asked with malice. Who dared to do such a thing?

They looked between each other, fear etched into their features.

"Answer me!" I yelled. They both flinched at the sound.

"The girl," they whispered.

My teeth ground together with such force my jaw felt like it was going to break into pieces. "What girl?" I spat the words out.

"The one that had the strange power, my queen."

"Niya," I hissed between clenched teeth.

They nodded. "Yes."

"I was told she was dead."

"We thought so your majesty. Reports state that she is in the forest."

I tilted my head slightly. "With followers?"

"Yes," they said quietly.

"How did she get followers?"

They shook their heads. "We don't know. We are getting more information for you. However, there is something else you should be made aware of."

"What?" I screamed.

"She's not alone."

I glared at them. "Obviously, you just said she had followers."

"We mean Marcus, my queen. Along with the old advisor Theo. They have accompanied her."

I could feel my blood boiling within my body. My veins pushing their way through my skin, my eyes bulging out as fury overtook me. In a voice that was more furious growl than human response I ordered the two men to gather my army at once. To fetch the elementals from the basement and send for my drakyn. "Do it now. I want them in the dirt by the end of the month."

They nodded with downcast eyes as they darted from the room. I looked across the long old wooden council chamber table to where the Azzarian king's council chair sat. The seat that Marcus had once occupied. Then my eyes flicked to the smaller chair. "I will have your head and your queen's on my gate. That I promise you."

Chapter Fourteen

Time passed in a blur. It was hard for me to keep track of everything that needed to be done. From moving people into proper formation, to making sure they were prepping themselves as best as they were able to. Most of all, the most difficult part was trying to figure out what the next step was.

Marcus had talked to Annabelle when we first arrived in the ruins of the Old Forest, hoping that Kaia had given her a shred of information to pass on to us. But unfortunately, she hadn't. That had been slightly disappointing, however Kaia had already helped me realize I needed Aleera. Kaia had done her part in helping, it was time for me to do the rest.

Marcus, though, was angry with Kaia. He didn't understand why she had sent Annabelle here. She came here with James to help, whether that involved staying back at the main camp and tending to the wounded or making food, anything to take some of the burden.

His very loud and vocal opinion was that she should have stayed in Azzaria, tending to their children. Not here.

He was obviously frustrated by her presence. The tension between the two was unpleasant, and I avoided them at all costs. But even that was not enough as their fights echoed throughout the camp most nights.

He also grew frustrated by the lack of direction that Kaia had provided. I understood why he wanted to be upset, but at times I wondered if he was mad at himself and taking it out on everyone else. I was okay with Kaia not telling us every step of the way things were meant to be. I was fine with figuring it out for myself. For me at least, it put less pressure on us.

Not knowing in the end what would happen. Just hoping that we made the right decisions at the right time. That fate would decide how it would play out, preferably in our favor.

We conferred with men and women who had been fighters prior to this current war. We asked for their expertise in determining what steps Tatiana would be most likely to take, would she strike here or there, what force could she bring against us, and most importantly, what could we do to make the odds be in our favor.

No one wanted to say it out loud, but fighting was truly just a guessing game. Who could predict their opponent the best, did she know me more than I knew her? Her tactics? I hoped I wouldn't be caught off guard twice.

Once we knew for certain her army was on the march a few days away and moving towards our position I had to bid farewell to James once again. He and the other ship captains would sail out to make a blockade between the islands of Aquaen and Azzaria.

Should Tatiana's ships attempt to get close enough to the shore to use their cannons or release any other nasty surprises, the hope was that they could take them out first or at least buy us some much-needed time. Those ships had carried many people from Azzaria and the other lands to here.

I didn't want to be the one to put the ships in harm's way, but the captains had volunteered and wouldn't be persuaded otherwise. It would be beyond difficult to lose some of them, but I knew there was a huge chance that Tatiana would give us everything she had at her disposal.

So, James left the ruins on his ship. He wasn't thrilled about it but with a light peck on the cheek, he made me a promise that he would be back. I couldn't give him such promises. Not when I had seen good people taken way before their time. I gave James a curt smile and hoped that we would both see it through to the end, that I would see him again.

After I watched him walk away, I went back to the others, and we began to make plans. Night after night, plan after plan, talk after talk, there was plotting, which grew old, and I grew restless. I wanted to get out there and do something, not sit around on my hands with a bunch of old men chit chatting about things that could perhaps happen or could never come to be.

She could choose to go around and flank us. Or perhaps she would send her whole army against us on the backs of drakyns. Who knew what was best? All we could do was protect ourselves and leave the rest in fate's hands.

I was resting far away from anyone else, alone in the ruins. I stared up at the shining stars in fascination as I laid on my back in the grass. I wondered if there were other places like Tileon having problems like the ones we faced. If there was someone far away, staring back at me.

I just watched the stars sparkle as I floated between dreams and reality. When a familiar smell permeated the air, I scrunched up my nose at the unwelcomed odor and slowly sat up to look around. That's when I heard numerous voices in the camp shouting fire.

"Fire?" I whispered to myself. I finally got a hold of my wits and stood up. "Shit."

The air in the distance was a cloud of black and gray that spread out with the wind. It was indeed a fire, if that's what you could call it, it looked more like an immense blaze.

I stared in disbelief at what I was seeing. It was the beginning of the night, darkness had just set over the forest, yet the sky was pink and orange above the treetops and the air was clogged with smoke. Ashes flew around in the breeze like little pieces of snow drifting lazily about.

People began to panic at the sudden turn of events. I watched frozen in place as they screamed and ran from the flames. It took a moment for me to understand what was occurring.

When realization hit me, I grabbed my stuff quickly and darted off in an attempt to keep order. I shouted at the top of my lungs, hoping to be heard. "Everyone to the middle of the ruins. Stay away from the tree line. If you are able to, take cover behind the buildings and get your weapons at the ready. We don't know what's about to come our way."

They slowly headed for what little cover was available, as the smoke began to get worse and worse. The distant cries of drakyns carried over the smoky air.

Marcus came running up to me. "What is going on?"

I tossed him an incredulous glare. "If I had to venture a guess, I'd say Tatiana is burning down the fucking forest around us."

"Tell me you're kidding."

"Do I look like I'm joking?" He looked around wide eyed. "I don't know why you're so shocked. She burned down Aquaen, why not burn us too?"

Others who were considered leaders to their people came over to Marcus and me. "My queen, what are your orders?" They all looked at me expectantly.

I swallowed down any doubt or fear I had left. The war was about to begin, I didn't have time to hesitate. "For now, we try to keep to the ruins to stay protected. They could come up behind us, so keep watchers in the forest as long as possible at a safe distance. Then get your fighters ready, for in an hour, we are going to march towards that fire and towards her army."

They nodded and went about relaying the orders. I looked at Marcus. "You need to find Theo. You two will be in charge of the army down here. You'll need to disable any archers or long ranged weapons first. Then finish off any elementals if there's some left alive."

He seemed alarmed at the words. "What do you mean if there's some left alive?"

"Me and Aleera are going to do everything within our power to deal with the drakyns and elementals, but I can't guarantee we'll get them all on the first sweep. So be careful. They're strong and have been trained to show no mercy to their opponents. It won't be easy to take them down."

He sighed heavily. "I know. You should be careful though. Tatiana's drakyn may be smaller than Aleera but those drakyns from Pyron were born with a coldness in their heart and the taste for blood."

"Aleera is older than you know. She has my back and I have hers. I trust that she'll protect me."

He enclosed my upper arms with his hands. "We'll get

through this, you and I." He squeezed slightly and I knew he meant it in a reassuring manner but for me it was anything but.

I nodded awkwardly. "Right. You should hurry, you have a long walk ahead of you."

He grinned. "They seem to be closer than we anticipated. At the end of the day Azzaria will be ours again."

I gave him a weak smile and turned around, heading towards Aleera. "I hope so."

I walked over to her and found her watching the smoke billowing high into the sky. The fire line grew larger in the distance. *"They're burning Mageia. I knew this forest well, it has been here longer than Tileon ever was. Before I even had a name."* She stared sadly at the destruction.

I didn't know how to comfort her. The loss for her had to be difficult to understand. "I'm sorry. Truly I am."

"Things come and go. Lands change, scenery changes. People change. It's inevitable," she said matter of fact. *"But still, it's hard when it happens, especially when it's right before your eyes. Are you ready for this?"*

I shrugged. "As much as one can be. Are the other drakyns?"

I wasn't sure if drakyns could smirk or smile. But I felt if they could, she'd be smiling now. *"Oh, yes, they are ready. It's time, my dear Niya."* She put her head down to the ground to make it easy for me to crawl upon her back once more.

I firmly gripped her scales and sat upright. I belonged here. It felt right to me, and I knew this wasn't the first time I had sat here during a battle. I stroked her iridescent scales trying to calm her and myself as I did my best to steady my nerves.

"Let's go." She launched herself quickly into the sky.

Wings beating as if to a drum, or perhaps it was more like a thundering heartbeat, she roared into the still ashy air. Behind us the other drakyns launched into the sky. They didn't fly as fast Aleera did.

We swirled above Marcus and Theo. Our army had started their march towards Tatiana and whatever horrible things she had in store for us.

The army moved through the tree line as we flew above them. We rose higher in the sky, hoping for the ability to see what we would be facing in combat. I squinted my eyes, barely able see her army and what I assumed was Tatiana. Flames illuminated the outlines of the drakyns she commanded.

At the front of the line were about half a dozen figures who were her elementals. A couple of them were setting fire to the forest that had once been home to the great nation of Mageia. Home to magic and wonder. It was now being burnt like kindling in a fireplace.

I felt a red-hot rage. This was my home, and it was going up in a fiery blaze before my very eyes.

"Aleera, tell the other drakyns to disarm or kill the elementals if it becomes necessary."

Her voice echoed in my mind. *"You wish them to die?"*

"No," I said immediately. "Only if it becomes necessary." I hesitated. "If it does become necessary, they need to do whatever it takes to bring them down."

"As you wish." A strange sensation tickled at the back of my mind as I felt her relaying the message along the bond. A painful buzz of the other drakyns' minds flowed back all at once. They weren't pleased that I wanted to spare the elementals and the other drakyns Tatiana had under her control. They wanted to maim and kill them in vengeance for what had happened in Tileon.

It took Aleera releasing a part of her power for them to agree to control themselves. I wanted to restrain myself, I didn't want to order the death of so many just because of who their ruler was. It didn't feel right, but war never does. It could come down to being as ruthless as she was.

I pushed that thought away and focused on my surroundings. Mainly how Aleera's wings beat to the rhythm of my heart as we flew into battle.

The coming dawn illuminated the battlefield as we approached Tatiana's army. The men and women on the ground stood opposite from one another. Staring each other down as drakyns in the sky hovered above to take stock of the battlefield.

Tatiana had more drakyns than we anticipated, but they were much smaller than ours. Would that be an advantage for us or them? I also noticed they had more elementals than we had been aware of, at least two dozen of them.

I wasn't proud of it, but I started to feel scared, not just for myself but for everyone. The elementals and drakyns would decimate the people we had standing with us. I couldn't think of that, not right now.

Aleera's words came to me. *"Caleb had a small army and it felt like it was him against the entire world. He felt hopeless almost every day. However, in the end, he made it through."*

She was right. He had accomplished his goal to free his people and Tileon. He won even when the odds were stacked against him. The odds were not stacked against us. We had older, wiser beings. We had men and women who were fighting for their lands. For their lives, their children's. They had a greater will and desire to fight, especially until the bitter end. And they had me.

I was startled when a horn blast trumpeted. It shook the air forcefully, causing my armor to rattle. It was a signal to their army that it was time to attack.

The men on the ground rushed violently at each other, weapons drawn. Swords clung upon swords, arrows whooshed into the air in the hopes of hitting flesh.

The flames of the fires illuminated the forest in the darkness. The fire elementals were burning people to a blackened crisp before they had the chance to draw blood. Large rocks were thrown into the fray, crashing into limbs and breaking bones. Numerous people began to clutch at their throats, scratching wildly, unable to scream out their final words as the very air was whisked from their lungs. Water rushed throughout the battlefield, washing people away without a trace.

I called out to Aleera. "We need to help them." My voice came out panicked, I knew I had ordered that the elementals be only disarmed but mass amounts of my people were being slaughtered. I wanted it to cease quickly.

She dove down immediately, rushing in to attack the elementals. Purple flames flew from her mouth, incinerating them in an instant. Behind us the other drakyns from Arcadia did the same, diving to the ground to pick off those who would harm our army. Though unlike Aleera they choose to eat the burnt soldiers.

The elementals stopped attacking the fighters on the ground. Instead, they began focusing their gifts of power on the creatures in the sky. They didn't show any prejudice to which ones they attacked. If it moved in the sky, they attacked it.

Blood soaked deeply into the greedy dirt as men tore each other apart and drakyns grappled with elementals. The scene made my stomach churn in utter disgust. How sad was it that this is what Tileon had been reduced to? How many lives were being lost for such a petty reason? I didn't want to dwell on it, I couldn't. Not at this time while bloodshed surrounded me.

Aleera roared loudly, agreeing her sentiments with mine. More purple flames erupted from her mouth as I tightened my grip on her scales with my bad hand. My forehead and eyes scrunched together tightly. In the distance I spotted what I had been looking for, the person who had plagued me for the last few years of my life.

The person I blamed everything on. Alec's death, the loss of Caleb, my brokenness. All because she wanted absolute power. Her greed had cost me so much, cost Tileon deeply. I was ready to face her again.

There, upon a blood red drakyn whose talons had ripped deep into my flesh, sat Tatiana. I couldn't tell what emotions passed on her face from this distance, but I could sense her eyes locked on to mine. I knew only of my own emotions, my unhealed scars and rage. Aleera felt my emotions as they flowed through the bond.

She knew my intentions, and she took it upon herself to fly towards Tatiana and her drakyn with purpose.

Chapter Fifteen

The two drakyns crashed violently into each other. Dagger length talons, shiny scales, and razor-sharp teeth collided together in a chaotic frenzy. Blood spewed in every direction, spraying across my face and raining down into the Old Forest.

Aleera sank her teeth deep into the smaller drakyn, tearing cleanly into the crimson scales. The smaller one pawed her hind legs at us. They shredded Aleera's legs, the sharp talons cutting easily into her flesh. Both creatures roared out from the immediate pain.

My eyes found Tatiana, she sat not far from me, a look of crazed madness plastered on her cruel features. She was screaming something, but over the sound of the two drakyns warring against each other, it was hard to make out exactly what was being shouted.

I was afraid. Not of Tatiana but for Aleera, I was terrified she was going to be seriously injured. Tatiana's drakyn screeched and hissed wildly, it drew blood with a fevered madness. It was coming at her as if this was the last meal that it would ever have in this lifetime.

I had to do something for Aleera's sake. The smaller drakyn landed a swipe at Aleera's right wing, tearing a small hole in it. My mind went to a dark place, what if it hurt her more, ripped up her wing so badly that she could never fly again? I couldn't allow that to happen.

In an instant, I made an impulsive decision. No second thoughts. No questioning if it was right or wrong. I gripped my hands as tightly as I could onto Aleera's scales as I stood up on her back. I bit my lip hard, hoping against hope that I didn't accidently slip on the slick blood and fall to my death.

Tatiana's eyes widened in shock as I leapt from Aleera's back to the red drakyn Tatiana controlled. It let go of Aleera and flew away from her at the sudden pressure from my body weight, but it was already too late.

I pulled my blade from its sheath on my back and held it aloft as I stared into the dark eyes of the Pyron queen. I plunged my sword hilt deep into the soft neck of her drakyn. It let out an ear-piercing shriek as agonizing pain took control of its mind. It began to flail around erratically, trying desperately to rip the blade from its neck to alleviate the pain.

It was stuck in between its scales; the drakyn's warm blood coated its crimson hide. It was unsuccessful in its attempts to dislodge the sharp metal. It was too late, its life's blood was pouring out in a river.

Tatiana clutched tightly to its neck as we started to plummet quickly to the ground. Before we hit the tops of the trees, I grabbed hold of my sword and freed it from the drakyn's neck, then jumped away from its tumbling body. I didn't want to risk the drakyn's body crushing me under its soon to be dead weight.

I plummeted freely and smacked into a couple trees,

crushing a few dozen branches on my way down. They surprisingly softened my landing more than I expected. I roughly plopped into a messy heap on the ground. A groan of pain from the fall escaped me and gave myself a once over, making sure I hadn't hurt myself too badly. I seemed to be okay, just a few cuts and potential bruises.

Off to my left, not far from me, I could hear the drakyn still gurgling on its own blood in agony. But its shrieks slowly began to die away as its life was finally gone from this world.

I stood up, my head dizzy and my body adjusting to now being on the ground. I wasn't alone, Tatiana was here as well. She presented as an easy target, or so I'd hoped.

I walked over to where her drakyn now laid lifeless, its warm blood still pooling on the ground. Its wings were shredded from falling through the sharp branches. I tried to hear its mind, but I couldn't hear any buzz of thought coming from it anymore.

A part of me was upset seeing it dead. It didn't deserve to die like this. If it'd had a different master, things could have ended so much differently for the poor beast. Just another life tainted by Tatiana's decisions. I needed to find Tatiana. I ran around desperately trying to find her. When I did at last, she was lying on her side in the dirt.

She stared daggers at me, small cuts marring her beautiful yet cruel features. Her eyes were filled with a furious rage, yet she smiled with smugness.

"I was so close the first time we met to claiming your life. You won't walk away so easily this time." I realized just then that she wasn't alone. Four figures appeared from the trees to come to her aid—the same elementals from the throne room.

My heart sped up as fear took hold of me. I could hear

Aleera suddenly in my mind. *"You're more powerful than them. You have nothing to fear from them. I'm here for you, Niya."*

Her words were a comfort to me in that moment. "No, *you* won't walk away this time. I'm stronger than I was before."

She scoffed. "We'll see."

"Yes, we will," I replied with little emotion. I couldn't have anything clouding my mind. This time the four didn't hold back. It wasn't one on one like at the palace, this time it was all four on one.

It took all my power to protect me. I leaned into the fact that I was a Vayu. The artifact of the Vayu. An ancient powerful being encased in flesh. I was beyond what these elementals were capable of, and while I knew they were extremely well trained, they were probably powerful in their own right, maybe could've been Vayus had they trained with the Maesters.

I would not be broken by fighting against them again. My body knew what to do and it had a mind of its own. My soul had fought in many wars and battles over the course of centuries. I had fought for years in the fighting pit. I'd fought to survive over and over again, something I didn't realize I would treasure in the future.

I had held a petty grudge towards Tyrone as, night after night, I was forced for hours on end to fight for gold. Now I understood that fate had put me on this particular path. I needed those skills for this moment.

I quickly ducked away as large rocks were hurled over my head. They flew past me to collide into trees that were somewhat intact for now. They smashed into the blood-soaked dirt, sending debris flying into the air.

In a distant part of my mind, I told Aleera to keep any

other elementals and any other drakyns that would dare to interfere at bay. This was my fight, not theirs. I wanted, no needed, to do this on my own. She obeyed my wishes, attacking anyone who came near.

Aleera even kept Tatiana corralled close by us, though she didn't look afraid of her current predicament. She merely watched while still lying on the ground with a gleeful look plastered on her face—perhaps in the vain hope that I would finally die, no longer a thorn in her side.

I felt the warmth seconds before flames licked up my flesh. Intense heat spread across my body, but this time it didn't turn my skin into a blackened crisp. I was able to protect myself like I had so many years ago with the fire elemental in the fighting pits.

The female fire elemental's flames weren't touching my skin. It was almost like I had a thin barrier over my body. The same occurred with the other elementals, their abilities washed over me, burning the ground and the plant life behind me.

I stood there in a daze for just a moment, letting it sink in that I was okay this time. I looked at the woman sending wave upon wave of flames my way and smiled.

"Not this time," I whispered. I blasted a bolt of pure raw power from my left hand. It shot out from my fingers like purple lightning and was accompanied by a white-hot flash of light. The power reached her rapidly and blew a massive hole into her chest. I could see the scenery through the gaping wound. She toppled down face first into the dirt, the edges of the hole black and still smoking.

It was at that exact moment I knew things had changed. Tatiana's smug smile slowly faded away, concern clouding her features as she still laid prone on the ground.

I kept hold of my sword as I darted around the earth

elemental. He desperately tried to swallow me into a hole he created in the ground. I used my magic to push the hole back towards him, sucking his body into the black pit in the dirt. He fell in and the hole closed around his shoulders, exposing only his head.

His eyes held an unspoken plea. Was it for mercy or death? I swiped my blade's edge along his throat, he cried out for a second as his blood spread onto the mossy undergrowth. His head went limp before the ground swallowed him completely.

The whole thing only took a few minutes, but you wouldn't have even known he was there in the first place. He was now just a mound of blood and soil with wildflowers slowly creeping in to cover it up, making something ugly now beautiful.

My eyes flicked to the two remaining elementals. They turned on their heels to run. Tatiana, however, was not having any such behavior. She screamed at the top of her lungs at them to turn and fight immediately.

I wasn't sure what she had done to them to make them fear her more than they feared me. Maybe it wasn't fear that forced them to turn and face me. Perhaps it was the promise of true freedom. Freedom from the horrific deeds they had done. They would be free to no longer live with the guilty conscience they carried. No longer under the rule of Tatiana and Pyron.

Water engulfed my body as air was sucked harshly from my lungs. I remembered the unpleasant feeling from my time spent in the ocean. Vivid memories flooded to the front of my mind and before I knew it, panic overran everything within me. I could feel myself slipping away. My control, my composure, my confidence.

Then hearty laughter filled my ears. I was pulled back

to my time aboard the Mischief with the pirate captain who saved me from sure death. A man who understood why I was scared to return to Tileon but still stood by me every brutal step of the way. He had fished me from the water and helped me heal. I wouldn't be standing here if it wasn't for him.

I pulled more memories from the dusty places I'd stored them. The feeling of dying slid away to the background. Instead, I focused on all the good I'd experienced in my life.

The warmth of friends, their unconditional love, of giggling until our bellies hurt by the fire as I made weapons with Alec. The moments we shared in Heka. The time I spent with Caleb and the rebels in the Old Forest. All the jokes that were told to keep spirits cheery.

The acceptance I felt aboard the Mischief, those people who would normally be called outsiders. They didn't judge me, they were like family. Even if they weren't my blood. They had found me, and I found them.

I couldn't disappoint them, I couldn't die here like this. I held on to that tightly, clutching onto the tether that held me here.

I pushed away the water surrounding me with a blast of pure magic. The two elementals flew back dozens of feet. They landed with a thud, gasping for air. While they were disoriented, I quickly walked over to them to end their time in Tileon for good.

My sword slid into the water elemental swiftly. His pale blue eyes met my purple ones, his filled with relief as he took his last breath. I glanced toward the female air elemental, her eyes widened as I blasted her with white hot light, reducing her to a mere pile of ashes.

I stood there momentarily, staring at the dead figures.

In a way I was sad it had come down to this. But there was one more thing left for me to do.

I turned my head to search around. There Tatiana laid crumpled on the ground in a blood red top and pants designed for riding a drakyn. Her long raven hair was pulled back tightly, yet stray wisps escaped from the pony-tail. The cruel angles of her face took on an eerie cast in the early morning light as she looked up at me.

Her chest heaved but it wasn't in fear. She wasn't frightened one bit, only annoyed at my presence. She opened her mouth to speak. "Do you think this will change anything? We will always want power. It's what we were made for. We weren't all meant to be equal. Perhaps you and I are equal in some regards. But Marcus and those other kings? They are hardly our equals."

I shook my head. "That's not the point. What you did isn't excusable."

She smiled. "You don't deny it. You know you are better, stronger than them. You were born to rule coun-tries. Yet you have to be seated next to a man who can't get his shit together."

"I'm not sitting next to anybody. It's just me," I stated simply.

"That's my point. You are the one who commanded this army, who made the choice to stand against me. Marcus did not have the strength to do such a thing. He scurried away like a rat into the night. He wasn't even the one who tried to escape the palace. No, it was that crafty Landen. If it wasn't for him, Marcus would have had his head on a spike long ago. Or he could have begged for mercy from me. He would've made a fun toy to play with. Wouldn't that have been interesting?"

I gave her a dark look. "He is stronger than you think."

She smirked at that. "Sure, he is. You keep telling yourself that, my dear Niya. This doesn't end with me. Others will rise up in my name to honor me."

I swallowed hard as dread filled me at the thought. "I hope for your people's sake that is not the case."

"I must admit I expected to have longer."

I looked down at the ground. "We always expect our days to be longer than they end up being."

"Isn't that the truth." She tilted her head. "I didn't expect you here. I thought I had ended you a long time ago."

"You almost did, you came closer than anyone else."

She smiled a feline grin. "I broke you. That's enough for me."

My mouth turned into a grim line. "Almost. You almost did, but I realized I was only bent, not broken. You came damn close to killing me, something I won't allow to happen again."

I dropped my sword and reached down with both of my hands to grab hold of her. When my grip tightened on her blood splattered top she began to struggle, clawing at my arms and face. Her nails went deep into my skin, drawing blood.

She screamed for me to get off of her, but her words fell on deaf ears. I took a firm grip with my good hand, making sure she couldn't escape. Her face was a mask of pure terror, her eyes as wide as saucers as she watched me.

"I've been wanting to do this for a long time," I stated coldly. I lowered my voice for only her to hear. "Not for Azzaria. Not for the countless deaths that lie solely at your feet. This is for taking him away from me. This is for Alec."

Before she could mouth a reply, I had taken my right

hand that now held a broken arrow, an arrow I took from a skeleton, and plunged it deep into her throat. I released my hold on her, she wobbled around in a daze scratching at her neck.

Blood poured out of her red lips, foamy as it dripped down her chin. She fell to the ground and struggled to breathe. She tried to inhale any air she could, but it was a useless endeavor.

I stood over her and watched as she took her last breath. I felt an odd satisfaction that she was gone. A life for a life. I closed my eyes and released a breath of relief that I had been holding onto.

I once more looked at her. Her orange eyes stared up at a smoke-filled sky. The arrow that had taken Alec away from me protruded from her neck. I bent over her dead body and with the tips of my fingers, closed the Pyron queen's eyes.

Chapter Sixteen

The fighting raged on all around me. No one took notice of the four dead elementals. What's one more dead body when there were already so many? Nor did they notice that the woman they had been fighting for was currently lying dead on the ground.

No one noticed her death. They hadn't had time to grasp her loss or understand what it meant for them. Her soldiers still fought against those of us who merely wanted freedom. Men and women who were survivors. As far as I was concerned, the war was over. For the others there was still fighting yet to be done.

I screamed out for Aleera. "Why haven't they stopped?" I asked stupidly.

"When war is being fought, soldiers are engrossed in their task. They don't usually take notice when it is time to stop. For them, their focus is on avoiding getting hurt or fighting until their last breath. They aren't prone to taking a moment to stop and pause to look around."

I wiped ash and blood from my forehead. "Then we

will have to make them stop." She tilted her head ever so slightly as she dipped her head down, allowing me once more to climb upon her back.

Aleera quickly launched into the air, her strong wings slicing through the sky. My stomach twisted and turned as I remembered tumbling freely towards the ground on Tatiana's drakyn. My memories replayed the unpleasant experience. It made me queasy just thinking about it.

We soared above the battlefield. The trees barely hung on to their branches, the dirt in random piles that made for good cover, fires burned chaotically across the battlefield.

I watched in horror as water elementals on both sides drowned their victims, tiny icy tendrils silencing their victims forever. Fire users burnt the skin off of nearby men and women. Earth elementals hurled boulders and rocks in an attempt to crush people, some threw plain dirt into the eyes of those they were fighting. Small tornadoes formed randomly to suck people into the swirling wind.

I had never seen gory violence on this scale, so many people brutally murdering others. Some had looks of joy plastered on their faces, others held distant haunted looks of sadness.

I told Aleera to start separating the two armies from one another. She let out a loud roar, telepathically telling what few drakyns remained on Tatiana's side to stand down immediately. They heard her voice but ignored her order. They went right back to what they were doing.

I tugged on my magic, pulling on it, before I forced it out. I pushed my magic into the minds of the drakyns, commanding them to stand down. They shrieked in pain as my power overtook them. They finally stopped, taking flight into the smoky sky and abandoning the battlefield. They soared for the safety of their homeland.

Aleera wondered if we should pursue them, but I knew we had better things to do with our time. I chose to let them fly away, it wasn't worth the hassle to try to get them right now. I wouldn't be surprised if they were hunted down in the coming days.

Aleera and I soared closer to the ground than I felt was wise. But I screamed out over the sounds of swords and dying that everyone was to cease immediately. I ordered them to drop their swords for the war was now over.

Our army did as they were told, their weapons falling to the blood-soaked dirt. Smiles accompanied happy cheers as we flew above, announcing the good news. I spotted Marcus and Theo toward the front of the fray, both men covered in grime. They watched as we gracefully flew above them.

I shouted out to them, hoping they could hear me at this distance. "Tatiana is dead." Relief spread on their faces. They dropped their swords and held filthy hands up in a salute. Turning around, they began to give out orders for surrender.

Aleera and I came in for a landing. She found a spot and came down swiftly, resting on the ground. I got off her back, somewhat glad to be standing on my own two feet.

Marcus sprinted over to us, his face split into a wide grin. "Is she really gone?"

Theo and Marcus, along with others, watched me closely. I nodded once.

"Azzaria is free! Tileon is free!" he screamed. Shouts of pure joy echoed along the men as they cheered at the news.

Marcus turned back to me, a triumphant look in his eye. "What are your orders my queen?"

I was taken aback by his words. I wasn't sure if I was

ready to be called by that title, especially by him. Right now was not the time nor the place to correct him.

"We figure out who can be put into the dungeons for the time being and who is a lost cause. Send them back to their lands, if possible, for their kings to deal with them appropriately." He nodded and spread the orders out to various people standing close by.

He gave me a strange look. "What about you?" he asked.

I could hear Aleera's voice in my mind incessantly, urging me to do something. The whole time we'd been on the ground she had been mentioning it. "I have one more stop to make. I'll be back within the day. Stay safe while I'm gone."

He smiled at me. "I look forward to when you come back."

I didn't respond, my head focused on the task at hand. I went back to Aleera and returned to my spot on her back. We took flight once more, this time to Azzaria. She beat her wings as fast as she could. I pressed my eyes closed as I felt the push of the wind rushing by me.

The trip didn't take as long as I expected, which shouldn't have been a surprise that when on the back of a drakyn it was faster to get to the palace. A place I once called home.

Aleera flew above the palace before she landed in the garden area. She kept a watchful eye out as I slid off of her. I was struck by the fragrant scent of flowers blooming all around me. The sun shone down brilliantly as I stared out at the ocean calmly making waves against the cliffside.

I stormed towards the palace with purpose. I wasn't thrilled with the inevitable task I had, but Aleera had made a very valid argument for it. When I couldn't deny that she was right, I knew exactly where I was meant to go. Straight to the council room of the Azzarian palace. No one came out to confront me, either the soldiers abandoned their posts, or they were still out on the battlefield.

I wasn't sure what to expect when I entered the palace. The hallway was empty, and it set my nerves on edge to see the red and black hall devoid of life. My feet carried me to the council room, and I flung open the door to the chamber.

It loudly banged against the wall. The people inside jumped out of their seats, startled at my sudden presence. Once they had a moment to process their faces held looks of confusion and fear.

I slammed the doors shut behind me as I took in Tatiana's counsel. These were her advisors and people who had helped her during her reign of terror. Sitting across from me, at the far end of the table, seated in the ornate chair that was meant for me, was her husband.

He looked resigned to the fact that he knew what was coming, he knew what I was here for. He didn't have a single word to say to me. He merely sat there with a neutral expression as the different advisors and councilmen made a huge ruckus.

They each made heartfelt pleas and begged for mercy, stating that they were forced to do the awful deeds they did. Their words continued on in the pointless hope it would pull on my heartstrings. They were sadly mistaken. I wasn't going to be swayed by such things.

I kept my eyes glued on the king consort. I said nothing as I let out a burst of magic. It was a familiar feeling, I'd used my gift like this only a couple of times before.

White hot heat blinded everything in the room as I became pure energy. It lashed out wildly, my raw power being released into the room to destroy everything in its path.

A dull ringing sounded in my ears as I became myself again, weak flesh containing the chaotic magic once more. Multiple piles of ash covered the table and chairs throughout the room. I stared at one pile in particular, it sat in the smaller throne meant for the queen of Azzaria, a small crown laid next to the gray dust.

I sighed heavily. Aleera had given me the advice to make haste and kill Tatiana's husband and all her advisors before they received word of her demise. She feared they would get the idea to seek revenge for their queen's death. I wasn't certain that they would do such a thing, but I wasn't willing to take the chance.

If I was honest with myself, I don't think he would've done anything. I saw the look in his eye. He was beyond tired, and frustrated, and he had been ready for death. Or he just knew in the end he would die if she did. Who honestly would leave him alive? The risk was too great to make such a mistake.

I was grateful they hadn't produced any children. I knew in my heart I wouldn't have it in me to remove them from this world. A sick guilt lived inside me over the lives I'd taken in my life, I didn't need more on my conscience.

I stood silently in the council room a moment longer, needing a minute to gather my scattered thoughts. I took a deep breath and left the chamber. I went around the palace carefully and ordered any guards I came in contact with to lower their weapons. Their queen was gone and unless they wanted to join her, they were to remove their armor immediately.

A few made the choice to fall upon their sword,

wanting to join her in the next life. All the rest were more than happy to be done, to have everything finally be over. To have the opportunity to go home, wherever their home was. They had never wanted this war, but they also didn't want their families to die.

It finally felt like Tileon could breathe again.

Chapter Seventeen

Aleera and I departed Azzaria, leaving behind what I had done. Being the one to eliminate Tatiana's brother and her council was not something I wanted to do, but I knew Aleera was right. It was for the best to get rid of them, they wouldn't tolerate things going back to the way they were.

I kept telling myself it had been a necessary evil and sometimes in war, you had to get your hands dirty. I'd been forced on many occasions to take the life of someone who needed to be removed for whatever reason. I had done it in Heka and Fajro. I took a sick pleasure in those deaths, being the one to end their lives.

I hadn't done it on such a large scale, at least not on purpose. Somehow this felt different, or it was just everything catching up with me at once. The king consort's face flashed in my mind, the utter defeat written there and the lack of emotion when he knew the end was there to claim him.

I took a deep breath of the fresh salty sea air that was breezing around me from the ocean. I stood there silently, just inhaling it. I looked over to Aleera. "Almost time to go?" I asked her quietly.

She didn't say anything in words, but I could feel the buzzing of her mind. She wanted to comfort me, all I wanted was to put all this behind me. I just wanted to move on to something else. I was so tired of fighting, tired of all the blood and death. I wanted something more than this life.

For now, I pushed those thoughts and feelings into a dark void. A place that held everything I hadn't been willing to deal with. I set aside all of that, staring out at nothing in particular. There was still so much more to do before I could truly breathe easy again.

Aleera leaned her head down and I returned to my spot on her back, and we launched into the darkening sky. She took her time flying back to the ruins, giving me a moment to process everything. I needed to think of what came next, I never was good at doing that. I usually just did what felt right in that moment. I had to be certain of the path I wanted to travel before we got to where we were going.

A day later, we returned to the ruins in the Old Forest. I looked below us. Flying over the battlefield was difficult for me. The soldiers and others must've spent all the time I had been gone cleaning everything as best as they were able to do so.

They had gathered all of the fallen bodies and seemed to be figuring out a proper burial for them. The earth elementals made graves for those who wished to be buried. The rest were burned on a giant pyre.

People were paying their respects to their friends and

family, hoping their souls would find rest in the next life. I wasn't entirely sure if there was any rest to be found. I was aware that my soul came back repeatedly. Did others as well? Were we all born again in a never-ending loop or just certain ones? It was a question I wanted answered, but I didn't think those in Heka had such an answer or wanted to know.

Once we had landed in the forest, I got off Aleera, and she went in search of food. I spotted Theo in the distance helping soldiers with supplies. I didn't want to distract him from his work, but I asked if Marcus was okay. He gave me a curt nod and said for the most part. When he had a free hand, he pointed off to a space in the woods where he and Annabelle had gone to speak alone.

I didn't want to interrupt their alone time, but I also needed to speak to him on some urgent matters. I walked to the spot Theo had pointed and searched around the trees to find them. My eyes fell upon a scene that shocked me to my very core.

I stood there frozen, trying to process what I was seeing. My brain struggled to understand it. A lone figure remained motionless amongst the trees staring down at a body lying limply on the ground. Blonde hair spilled out in a circle around their head.

It was difficult to tell in the hazy light filtering through the branches, but in my heart I knew. I stared at the figure standing eerily still. Clutched in their hand was a long dagger coated in red, small drops of crimson liquid dripped off the blade to form a puddle in the dirt at their feet.

I whispered quietly, the word tumbling out in shock. "Marcus...?"

The figure turned around, startled at my sudden presence. He glanced down at the body. "I didn't realize you were coming back so soon."

My heart was racing. "I went to take care of things in Azzaria."

He nodded stiffly. "Making sure no one else would become an issue later. That's clever. Very clever and smart."

"What happened?" I asked carefully.

Marcus looked down at the body on the ground, then back up at me. His eyes not quite seeing her, but perhaps he did, I wasn't sure. "I had to do the same as you."

I looked at him, confused. "You had to do the same?"

"You said you had to go to Azzaria. To clean up and make things better for us."

I nodded woodenly. Out of habit, not agreement.

"She disagreed with me on so many things," he stated simply. "No matter what I wanted to do or try to do. She always felt that it wasn't quite enough, it wasn't right. She wasn't meant to be a queen, wasn't meant for this life."

I stuttered out a response. "J-Just because she wasn't b-born to be queen, doesn't mean she wasn't m-meant for this life."

He shook his head, seemingly more for himself than me. "You don't understand. She had changed into a different person, one that was angry and distant. The last five years had taken a toll on her, she buckled under all the pressure."

"No," I said quietly. "She wouldn't have wanted this. She didn't want to die Marcus. Not like this."

"How would you know?"

"She would want to see her children. Raise them in Azzaria out in the open."

His eyes floated down. "Perhaps, but it would have

been hard on her going back to the way it was. Trying to go back to pretending every day. Acting like everything was okay, like we were happy. Showing all of Tileon that our marriage was rock solid. It wasn't working."

"Because you guys lived in a sewer for five years while you attempted to raise two children. You both had to go through so much."

He shook his head violently. "No, that's not why. It's because we weren't actually married. You and I, however, were meant to be together. While we were apart, I should have waited for you." He turned fully towards me. "I'm so tired of pretending. I don't want to continue to pretend like my wife is someone else when it's you. I want to acknowledge you as my true wife when we return to Azzaria."

"Marcus…" I took a huge step away from him.

"Please…We tried, me and her, we did. But it was too much. All of what we went through together. It drove a wedge between us that neither of us could ever fix. She held onto the thought that she could just go live on the other side of the palace but think of how important a queen is to her people, to *our* people. The king and queen vote on things that we would constantly have to discuss together, important matters. What if we were not able to agree on things? I refuse to go through another incident like this one. This could have been stopped five years ago, had she listened to me, had she done what was right. She split us up and broke us permanently."

I looked down at the still form that had blonde hair spreading out from it. Her face was turned away from me. I closed my eyes and swallowed down the bile bubbling into my throat for just a moment before looking back at him. "No. I'm not interested in being queen of anywhere. I never asked for this life, I've never wanted it, but I agreed to do it for your sake and for Azzaria's sake. That time is long gone. I'm tired of fighting Marcus, I'm tired of this. I don't want to be your wife, I never did. I just want my life to be one I choose to have. No one else making the decisions for me. I've done everything that's been asked of me."

"This is what is meant to be, you and I, together," he said quietly.

"The Marcus I know would never ever do this to the woman he loved. To the mother of his children," I replied.

"The Marcus you knew died the day Tatiana stepped foot on Azzarian soil and accepted our surrender."

"I was married to that Marcus. I don't even recognize you anymore and I sure as shit don't want to know this version of you. You want to acknowledge me as queen of Azzaria? So be it. But I will never be your wife in any sense of the word, and should you ever try to make me, that knife is going to end up in your heart next." I gave him a cold look, daring him to argue with me.

Multiple emotions passed over his features. He landed on disappointed and upset. "So now what?"

"Now we talk about what's truly important for Tileon." The change in subject was a relief but I couldn't help my eyes from glancing at Annabelle and feeling sick.

He glared at me. "And what's that?"

I waved my hand around pointing at the forest. "This, all of this. Pyron started this war because they felt left out of Tileon. That they weren't wanted here."

He scoffed. "Boo fucking hoo. That's not my problem that they had their feelings hurt."

I gave him a dirty look. "That is your fucking problem. You're king of Azzaria for now and you need to stop pushing aside Pyron, they are a part of Tileon whether you like it or not. Going forward you have to accept them. You need to make them part of your people. Marry one of their daughters to your son or vice versa. Include them, for years you and the other rulers have left them out of everything. It's not a complete shock that they grew bitter and angry. No more! You have to include them, you have to accept that they are a part of this world. If you can't do that, then I will find a different King that will."

He narrowed his eyes at me. "Is that a threat?"

"No, it's a promise. I won't stand for you acting like one of the four lands doesn't fucking exist when it does. I won't have another war because of your hatred and stupidity."

He looked upset and glanced down. His eyes scanning his hands and the dagger he still held. Reluctantly he looked at me and uttered one word. "Fine."

"Fine?" I asked.

"I will do everything in my power to make sure they are included as a part of the new Tileon."

"I want your word Marcus, and you better keep it. For if you give me your word, it would be bound to my magic. Should you break your promise to me, it won't be pretty."

He gave a small nod. "You have my word, Niya."

I carefully and cautiously walked over to him. I didn't dare look down as I got close to the woman lying there. My stomach turned at the thought. I stuck out my hand, my mark glistening in the light. He moved the dagger from one hand to the other, he put the hand still covered in blood into mine.

He shook my hand in agreement. The moment his hand touched mine a wave of pure light exploded out of me. It wasn't a painful feeling, only a tingling numbing sensation. My knees almost went out underneath me. The only thing holding me up was Marcus's hand.

I said it out loud, but I must have also said it in my mind. "What the fuck was that?"

I heard Aleera's voice answer. *"Magic. You've brought magic back to Tileon. You should be grateful. For now, new elementals will be born in a world that is safe for them. The Maesters will seek them out to train them when the new elementals make themselves known."*

New elementals? I was surprised at the strange thought that this war ending not only freed Tileon from Pyron but brought back magic and elementals as well. What a strange thought.

Marcus looked at me. "Are you okay?"

I smiled. "I'm more than okay. We are finally at peace and the world has a bright future ahead of us."

The stone chair was firm and chilly underneath me as I heard another person come to me for help. Their desires were granted one by one as more and more came forward. They were farmers, soldiers, and people from the marketplace.

They came from all over begging for help from the king. I had done my best to make sure they were well taken care of as we slowly built the city back to its former glory. We had painstakingly scrubbed the blood from the streets, homes, and palace gates.

Though to my eyes the red stains still coated everything. I couldn't unsee the carnage. Even when I had all the artwork, drapes, and other heinous decor ripped down and burnt; some days I could barely walk down the halls.

I couldn't bear the sight of seeing pictures of Tatiana hanging from my palace walls. The home of my family and blood had been forever tarnished in my eyes.

I didn't let the little things bother me, or at least I tried not to. I sat on my reclaimed throne and attempted to be fair to all, not showing favor to any one person. I only gave them what they absolutely needed to rebuild their lives. It was slow drawn-out progress.

Yet the people were beyond happy. Their king had returned, all hail King Marcus, the protector of Azzaria and the man who brought peace back to Tileon. I was kind and just to my people, it wasn't time for a harsh ruler. Not after the last five years.

The people had cheered proudly for me not only in Azzaria but when we had marched into Pyron. We went into the heart of Pyron to free them. I had made an announcement in Fajro that their queen was dead. I was shocked that instead of anger, they had looked relieved. They wanted a different life and now they could have it.

The last three months had been torturously long. I was on a fool's errand to rebuild everything back to the way it was. Encouraging my people and the other lands to settle into a routine. Many had gone back to their work and once more resumed their daily lives, putting the past five years behind them.

Landen, Kaia, and the rest of his family had said their farewells to me and quickly gone back to what was left of Aquaen. They left with a team of water elementals to rebuild their land. It would take a few years to return it to the spectacular icy wonderland it had been, but it was worth the effort.

I missed the man. He grew on me during our prolonged time deep inside the sewers. I tried not to dwell on that time for too long. I didn't want to think of the foul stench that clung to me day after day. No, instead I now filled my nostrils with the sweet, clean, refreshing scent of the salty ocean air. The breeze brought an amazing smell to me every single day through the open palace windows.

I now watched my children play openly in the

sunshine of Azzaria. They ran and played happily through the lush green grass and wildflowers as they giggled with joy. Their life might have started literally in the trenches of shit, but it wasn't going to end that way.

The last citizen of the day departed the chamber, and I made my leave of the throne room. I needed my alone time, to sit silently in my study sipping on the rich dark liquid that helped ease the worries on my mind. I wasn't proud that I had turned to it, but most days it helped more than others.

For a while everything seemed to be going great. Then I would be blindsided with an irrational anger that simmered inside me. I was furious at Niya. With Annabelle gone, I assumed that we would rule together, side by side. With her next to me we would help Tileon heal.

Every night I would get to go to bed with her, get to caress her skin and have her as my wife in all the ways I'd dreamt of. Yet, she had rejected all my efforts to reunite us, a look of absolute disgust on her face when she told me no again and again.

In the study, I took a large swig of the amber liquid. I was trying to forget those magical purple eyes that had stared up at me with fire flickering in them as we sat in a cave and I pressed my lips to hers. Not a short peck on the lips but her mouth upon mine, my tongue entwining with hers.

Until she abruptly pulled away from me, telling me it was wrong, that it could never happen between us. My temper bubbled up, and I drained what was left in my glass and poured some more. I needed to dull my senses today.

I'd spoken extensively with Theo about my desire to

acknowledge Niya as queen. My hope was that by telling everybody who she was, the true queen of Azzaria, it would sway her to stay. Theo convinced me that it would do the opposite, it would only hurt my cause. Niya had made her intentions clear and once she set her mind to something there was no changing it.

So, I sat bitterly on a stone throne day after day alone. The chair next to me obviously empty, a constant reminder that I had lost not one but two wives in a way. I not only lost my queens but when Theo heard the news from Niya about what I had done to Annabelle, it apparently had made a decision for him clear as well.

The crumpled up scroll still sat in the corner collecting dust. Its contents were burned into my brain. The words stated that he no longer wished to be the royal advisor in Azzaria. After all these years, he wanted a change. Everything had been difficult for him, from losing my father, his close friend, to losing Annabelle, along with all the losses we had endured. He no longer felt the same about Azzaria and no longer wished to live here.

He had begun to say his goodbyes to everyone. I hadn't had the heart to say anything to him. No, I just let him go on his way. Especially now, as he chose to abandon me. I truly felt alone for the first time in my life. All I could do was take care of my son and daughter, making sure they were healthy and happy.

I'd keep myself strong for Azzaria's sake, but I would never forgive Niya or Theo for leaving me behind. Not when they were needed most. I drained my drink, putting those two in my past as I focused on my future.

I put the last piece of clothing inside my bag and pulled the tie shut. I glanced around the now barren room, taking in every detail. I'd spent an entire lifetime living here, but what did I have to truly show for it?

I had always considered myself a wise fighter. But what I hadn't realized was perhaps I was only physically strong. That mentally over the years, the fight had begun to drain everything from me. I felt an exhaustion I had never known existed.

Every day was an immense struggle to just get from one moment to the next. All those days we spent under the Swords and Sin took their toll on me. I constantly thought about how much I was done with everything. I was tired of royalty and the royal life, tired of the politics. Making sure not to step on anyone's fingers or toes. Bending over backwards to keep everyone happy.

I realized that's why I liked her so much. Niya was refreshing. She didn't give a rat's furry ass if you didn't bow low enough for her or call her by the correct term. No, she said what was on her mind and kept you honest, kept *me* honest. She had seen things she wasn't willing to talk about or discuss, and I respected her boundaries on that.

I never in my wildest dreams expected her to come to my tent and tell me a truth that shook my whole existence. She came to me the first night after the war ended, wanting to speak about Annabelle's death. Marcus told me she slipped and fell, hitting her head on a sharp rock before bleeding out. He lied and told me he wasn't able to do anything to help her.

I wanted to hold on to the softness in my heart. It would tell me to listen to him, to believe him, why would he ever lie about that? But something about the way she spoke, it held a harsh bluntness to it. Made you believe in whatever nasty reality she was telling you. It was the truth whether you liked it or not.

I knew his time in the sewers had changed him. I had witnessed and seen the arguments between him and Annabelle. I took the kids aside nearly every day so they wouldn't have to see too much of it. Yet I never thought it would come to this.

The last couple of months, something inside me became restless, it was a beast that wanted to crawl out of its cage. I ended up asking a friend for a favor, and he was more than willing to accept it. I felt like I tied up every loose end that I could. There honestly was no more for me to do.

I left behind the room I'd spent decades in, the room meant for the royal advisor. I was done being that person. I was no longer going to be addressed in a regal manner. I was just Theo now. Something about that was exhilarating.

I attempted to say goodbye to Marcus, but he refused to see me. I did the next best thing, I left him a letter explaining my intentions. Hoping that my reasonings were good enough for him but he held an anger in him that I did not recognize, and I didn't want to deal with it any longer.

I left the palace; I stood staring at it for a long time. A place I had called my home for so many years, or it had been before Tatiana twisted it into an unrecognizable city.

I was ready for a new adventure. I turned in place, my back towards the palace, and made my way to the docks.

Dust from the old tome flew into my face as I closed it. I gave a cough and tried to wave away the dust now floating in the air. I don't know why I decided to do this. Indulging myself with knowledge that wasn't necessary, it only hurt me. Yet here I was, I couldn't help myself.

I sat here in this musty library filled with light, but I found no joy in it. I read book after book about Caleb, about his life. He said absolutely nothing about our time together or how the war ended, just that it did, and he was suddenly king. There was a gap in the passages on what came next, it was quite some time before his next entry. The journals and recorded history of him wouldn't start again until almost two years later.

Those texts made note of when he and Brisa married each other. I was curious on what happened during those two years? Why nobody had any record of it. Why he never spoke of it in any of his detailed journals. He merely stated that the war ended and then two years later he had a wife who happened to be an air elemental.

Their time together was well documented throughout various books. All the different council meetings attended and laws they passed. They went on to have three sons, each a year or two apart from one another. From all the eyewitness accounts I read, it seemed like they had a very happy marriage.

It hurt to read such words. That he went on to have a

happy life, have a wife and sons. While I was here cleaning up a mess that should have never been made. It should've been me there with him. I hated that that was not fate's design.

I put the books back onto their shelves and left the library. I wandered aimlessly around the garden as I had done every day and night for the last couple of months. I walked up and down the paths that wound their ways over the expansive garden space. One of the smaller books I had read mentioned that the garden, waterfall, and orchard had been built in honor of Caleb's one true love. A selfish part of me hoped he built this in memory of me. Whether or not he did, just being here made me feel close to him.

I walked down to the paved area that ventured of into the cliffs. A place I had once jumped from to escape certain death. I watched the water calmly sway back and forth, it was peaceful today. Similar to the way Tileon and Azzaria had calmed down, at least as much as it could in such a short amount of time.

Everything had begun to change. I had reluctantly said goodbye to Aleera and the other drakyns. A month ago, they had flown away. Not back to Arcadia, as Aleera made clear to me, but somewhere else entirely new. I asked her if we would ever see each other again. She gave a hearty drakyn laugh and told me of course we would, we were destined to meet in another lifetime as we always did. I held a sad smile on my face as she left. I looked forward to seeing her again, however long that would be.

I spent a few weeks getting to know Kaia and Landen. I didn't know if I could ever fully thank them for all the things they did behind the scenes. If it hadn't been for Kaia, I would never have had the courage to do what I needed to do. She helped fix a broken woman and for that I was eternally grateful.

I was still a coward in other ways though. I hadn't gathered the courage to see Tyrone after my outburst in the sewer chamber. In my own way, I felt it was best for us to just leave things as they were. I'd stood in the alleyway watching across from the Swords and Sin one day. He had rebuilt the place for the most part, cleaned it up until it sparkled. But he had changed a lot of how he operated it. He lost his thirst for blood, instead throwing himself into weaponry and other such things. It was a surprising and interesting change, one I was proud of.

Theo had spoken to me on numerous occasions, telling me of his future plans. I was thrilled for him and slightly jealous. I knew he tried to speak with Marcus, in the hopes they could part as friends, but Marcus had refused to see him in any capacity.

Marcus had been willing to talk to me. I came to the throne room to discuss things, but all his words fell back onto one topic. All he wanted was someone to sit next to him, to help him through the rough coming years. He didn't want a friend, only a wife. He desired me for what I was, a princess of Mageia. It was the same thing he had wanted me for so many years ago. He didn't want Niya the person, only the title and what people thought of me. They looked up to the savior of Tileon.

I made a choice that day. To throw away all those titles that were given to me, the ones I'd earned. I was only Niya, nothing more. I left him in the throne room in a furious rage. Let him throw a tantrum on his own. I couldn't have cared less. I had finally made my decision and I couldn't wait to see where it would lead me.

. . .

I glanced around the bustling docks in search of something. I accidently bumped into a few people in my pursuit to find a ship that I was very familiar with. I finally spotted it and smiled, my stomach fluttering with butterflies. I walked up the main plankway, hearing orders being yelled out by the captain to his crew.

I stood motionless at the top of the plank waiting for a particular friendly face. A few minutes passed until ocean blue eyes noticed me, then the man turned fully to me with a huge grin on his handsome face.

"My lady!" James called out. "To what do I owe this pleasure?"

I gave him mischievous smile in return. "Permission to come aboard Captain?"

He chuckled. "Permission granted."

I stepped up on the main deck and walked over to where he was standing. "I have been thinking about something for a long time."

"Oh?" he said curiously.

"The last few years have been hard. I realized things for me have changed in so many ways. I've never felt like I could decide anything on my own."

"Okay…" he said, confusion crossing his face.

"Well, I finally have decided on something of great importance."

James looked at me expectantly.

I blushed as the words came out. "Is that offer still available? You know, the one for a girl who's looking for an adventure and freedom?"

His handsome features changed instantly into pure joy as he gathered me up into a tight hug. He let me go and just stared at me. "The offer definitely still stands."

"I want to take you up on it."

He nodded and gave me one more hug before returning his attention to his crew. Time went by in a blur as everybody went about their work getting the ship ready to leave its port.

I walked to the back of the ship as I felt the ship lurch forward. There was Azzaria falling away and fading into the distance, and I said goodbye to my only home. I felt fluttering in my belly once more. I gently placed my hand on my stomach, I had brought a piece of Caleb back with me. My magic had protected it even when I was unaware of its presence.

I smiled once more and turned around, leaving Azzaria behind me as I went to join Theo and James on an adventure of a lifetime.

Nicole Jamison (third person is weird) is a writer from the beautiful PNW. She originally is from a small town in Nevada (Carson City, though I rarely find anyone that knows where that is), where she discovered her fascination of supernatural stories (pirates, mermaids, and mummies, oh my!). She tends to lean into the dark side, finding love in dark twisted stories with morally grey characters that make her want to throw the book across the room (looking at you Vampire Academy and Night Huntress series). She also decided to just let the voices in her head say whatever they want and embrace it (sorry, Mom). She has two kids she loves more than anything (though they are not allowed to read my books until I'm long gone, or I'll die of embarrassment), and a husband that gets her dark humor and weird side. When she is not writing she is baking cookies or working in her garden (trying to get the spoils of my labor before the squirrels do).

She hopes you love her stories and characters as much as she does!

Keep up to date with Author Nicole Jamison on the latest news and upcoming books!

facebook.com/authornicolejamison

instagram.com/authornicolejamison

tiktok.com/@authornicolejamison